Placement One:

Fae Audits

G Clatworthy

ISBN: 978-1-915516-70-1

1 2 3 4 5 6 7 8 9 10

Cover art by Get Covers.

Published by G Clatworthy
www.gemmaclatworthy.com
gemma@gemmaclatworthy.com

Manufactured by IngramSpark
Australia: Ingram Content Group AU Pty Ltd, Melbourne, Victoria.
US: Lightning Source LLC, La Vergne, Tennessee / Allentown, Pennsylvania / Jackson, Tennessee, United States.
UK: Lightning Source UK Ltd, Milton Keynes, United Kingdom. Europe: Lightning Source UK Ltd, with facilities in Germany, France, and Spain.

The authorized representative in the European Economic Area for EU GPSR is Lightning Source France
1 Av. Johannes Gutenberg, 78310 Maurepas, France
compliance@lightningsource.fr
This book was manufactured using paper and ink products in accordance with commercial standards.

Foreword

This book is for anyone who's ever felt like they're working for vampires!

A special thank you to my amazing typo hunters, grammar gurus, and plot pickers who got this story to where it is today. You are awesome!

If you want to support Gemma, you can find her on patreon for exclusive first reads of new stories. You can also join her newsletter for free stories at www.gemmaclatworthy.com and follow Gemma on www.instagram.com/gemmaclatworthy, www.facebook.com/gemmaclatworthy or join the reader's group on facebook: Gemma's book wyrms. And grab a free prequel to the Vampire Graduate Scheme series here: https://books.gemmaclatworthy.com/vampire-graduate-scheme-prequel

Chapter 1

Nothing frightens me. After one is changed so dramatically, everything else pales by comparison. I can remember when I first decided to take a risk on myself, when I realised that I had the power to change my fate and that of others. That's how the idea for the Bathory Corporation began; with a desire to embrace change and never be afraid again.

Elizabeth Bathory – *The First Disrupter*

Coffee seeped through my suit sleeve giving me a patch of warmth that turned frigid within seconds.

"No. No, no, no." Not today. I tugged at the jacket and mashed a tea towel at the damp patch.

"Well, you can't wear that now." Abby – my flatmate and stater of the obvious – gestured at the stained suit.

"You think?"

"Get changed."

"Into what, Abby? This is my only suit," I snarled.

My flatmate disappeared into her bedroom. I sighed. My snapping was another sign of how much this meant to me. The last chance I had to get on a graduate scheme and start earning my way out of my student loan debt. If I didn't get a spot, I'd have to reconsider the minimum wage offer that the local supermarket had made, and accept that a kid from the foster system couldn't make it big and all my hard work had been for nothing. And I'd be stuck here in Cardiff instead of moving to London with Abby.

"Sorry, Abbs." I called after her contritely. It wasn't her fault I was a mess.

She reappeared holding up a suit hanging from a padded clothes hanger. "No dramas. Wear this."

I gaped at the purple suit. It was about as far from my grey and black colour palette as possible. But I didn't have a choice. It wasn't like I had a spare suit hanging in my flat pack wardrobe.

I scuttled into my bedroom to grab a new white shirt – they had come in a pack of two – and changed, doing up the buttons as I walked back out for the skirt suit. I pulled it over my thin frame and looked in our hall mirror.

The skirt hung past my knees but didn't look too bad, and the plum colour set off my black hair well, but the jacket gaped over my chest and hung from my shoulders like I was playing dress up with my big sister's clothes. I pulled at it, rearranging the lapels, but it didn't help. Abby was curvy, and I was skinny, verging on scrawny.

"I look like an idiot." Behind me, a scratching sound came from my giant pet hamster. "You agree with me, don't you?"

Nibbles made a small squeaking noise before running back into his guinea-pig sized plastic house.

"Don't listen to him, Elle. He's a hamster." Abby cocked her head to one side and tapped a painted nail on her jaw before darting into her room. When she reappeared, she held a gold belt that she wrapped around my waist, unbuttoning the jacket so the poor fit was less noticeable. I looked back in the mirror. It was better and, more importantly, presentable for the assessment centre. She had a way with clothes that I didn't.

The only thing that stood out was my Lilo and Stitch watch, but I'd worn it every day of my life since I'd got the gift, and it would be my lucky charm today. Ohana means family, and I'd find my new family at work as soon as I got this job.

"OK, let's go." Abby snagged her colourful handbag from the table, and I grabbed my oversized black bag, checked I had everything for the fifth time and hung it from my shoulder. On the way out, I flipped the light switch and one of my spiralling thoughts gripped me. What if the lights burnt out because I hadn't switched them off properly and the fuse didn't trip and a rogue spark landed on our crappy sofa, which caught fire because the landlord hadn't bought something up to code and our flat burned down?

I know, it sounds crazy. I never said it was rational. I flipped the light switch seven times. The perfect number. And the fear subsided. I took a deep breath. Now I could leave the apartment.

Of all the days for a flare up, why today? I thought I had it under control. I *did* have it under control. Nothing bad was going to happen. I'd spilled coffee on myself. My bad luck was done for the day.

Abby kept quiet as I adjusted my bag. She'd accepted my quirks long ago, and the perk of living in a clean apartment outweighed my weirdness.

"Why are you coming with me?"

"Got to check you get there OK." Abby shot me a wink. "And I've got a present for you…"

I looked at her out of the corner of my eye, but she tapped her nose and sped on, her boots tapping on the tiled stairs as we made our way out of the building and onto the city street. My own four-inch heels scraped the ground; I was up on my tiptoes, unused to walking in heels despite wearing them to every interview since March. Now it was August. My university course was over, and, despite Abby's reassurances, I was worried about my finances. I was careful with my money, but a student loan can only last so long, and I was a hundred pounds over my overdraft limit.

I knew because my bank had sent me a stern letter about limits, repayments and interest rates. I could do the numbers. They were bad.

This was it. My final chance to make something of myself. I'd get this job, work hard and become a director in five years and never have to worry about money again, I'd be sure of myself, confident and certain of my place in the world. That was the plan, anyway. I checked my watch. Plenty of time.

Abby stopped in front of a coffee shop on the main street. I looked up at the blue painted sign; The Dragon's Head. I gave her a questioning look.

"What better way to make sure you slay with the vampires than with a dragon's help?"

My frown deepened, but I followed her inside. She ordered for both of us and waved away my offer of payment. "My treat," she said and added a shot of charisma to the order.

I rolled my eyes behind her back. Yes, magic was real, but shots of charisma or glamour in a coffee cup? Come on. The chirpy woman behind the counter whose name badge proclaimed her as 'Brinda' didn't even have any magic. I could always tell. She mixed in a shot of the supposed charisma potion from a glass bottle on a shelf. It was only a third full. I guess lots of people wanted to add some pizazz to their day.

"OMG!" Abby squealed. "Is that the princess?"

I turned to see a short, curvy redhead chatting with a tiny gnome with purple hair in the corner of the café. It could be Princess Amethyst; she was something of a celebrity in Cardiff after marrying an elf prince, but was it her? I squinted. Was that an axe under the table?

Someone in a suit barged past me, knocking me against the counter and making me forget about the weapon as I stumbled to keep my balance.

"Sorry," I mumbled automatically, focusing on the large knot in his silk tie rather than meet his gaze.

"What are you apologising for?" Abby asked. "Hey, jerk. You bumped into my friend."

The stranger looked Abby up and down before smirking. "I'd make it up to you, but I've got an interview to get to." He gave her a wink and headed for the door.

Abby took a step forward, but I held her back. "Just leave it."

She screwed up her face, itching to go after him.

"Please," I said.

"Fine. But you should stand up for yourself. You deserve to take up space in this world, and you shouldn't let people walk all over you."

"OK." That was the problem with having an agony aunt for a friend; she always had an opinion, and she was right ninety-five per cent of the time. I'd crunched the numbers one Saturday night during a fit of boredom.

Abby handed me my drink and we headed back into the street, now bustling with people on their way to work in neat uniforms. I sniffed the coffee. Behind the rich, bitter aroma was the sticky feeling I'd come to associate with fae. Maybe there was something in the drink.

"Is it right for me to take something that could improve my performance before an interview?"

Now it was Abby's turn to roll her eyes. "It's not like it's drugs – it's perfectly legal and everyone does it. You'll be at a disadvantage with the other candidates if you don't."

It was good logic. I sniffed again and took a sip. It was sweet and had a hint of cinnamon in the aftertaste. Not bad, but not something I'd rush to have again. I drank some more.

"I don't feel different. Do I look different?"

"It's a charisma shot, not a beauty charm. Hadn't you better get a move on?"

I checked my watch, gave an unprofessional squeak and jogged along, leaving Abby behind. I pulled up in front of the Bathory Corporation Cardiff office, out of breath and feeling sweaty. I paused before entering, tugging my suit jacket down with one hand as I took in the building.

The atrium was glass fronted, but the higher floors had smaller windows between stone pillars. This was an old building, and it had an air of wealth and power that spoke of permanence and belonging; it wasn't as flashy as the newer high-rises, as if it knew its place and its value to the city and had all the confidence that came with that.

I glugged down the last of my coffee – I'd take anything that could help me with this interview – and strode in, only slipping once on the polished steps.

My high heels clacked on the tiled floor, drawing the eyes of the other candidates waiting on the stuffed couches in the reception area below banners displaying the company's values: Bravery, Overachievement, Loyalty, and Drive. The acronym spelled BOLD, exactly what the Bathory company wanted.

I checked my watch again; just on time. A perky man behind the desk signed me in, gave me a pass with a Bathory Company logo of a bat in the centre of a shield – larger versions were stamped on posters across the lobby – and told me to find a seat.

I sank onto the padded cushion of a red sofa and smoothed my skirt out three times; the number I permitted myself in public, not as good as seven, but enough to soothe me. It was irrational, but I had the sudden belief that a wrinkle in my clothes could make me fail the interview. To distract myself, I pulled out the book I carried in my bag; an autobiography of Elizabeth Bathory herself.

The woman was an icon. I had briefly considered cutting my hair and dyeing it red to match her angular bob, but here, in her building, I was glad I hadn't given in to the urge. A sudden thought gripped me that it might look too desperate to read her book here, and I shoved it back into my bag. Instead, I tried to channel her energy as I pressed my skirt again. No fear. Boldness. Confidence. I was worthy of a place here. I deserved a place.

"You here for the assessment centre?" a soft-spoken, fresh-faced woman asked me. Her eyes were ringed with the perfect amount of black eyeliner.

I nodded. "You?"

She held out her hand. "Ariana."

"Noelle, but call me Elle." I shook her hand and weighed up whether I should ask her to be an ally in the team tasks today.

"You might as well go home." A tall man with an immaculate suit and a tie with an oversized knot said, crossing his long legs. "This late in the process, there's lucky to be one spot left. And it's mine."

"We've all got an equal chance," I said, annoyed that he could dismiss us all like that. And why did he look familiar?

He laughed. "Yeah right." Confident prick. But maybe he had a point. There were – I counted – thirty of us here and he was the only one without any outward signs of nerves.

Something clicked in my brain, and I knew where I'd seen him before. "You bumped into me at the coffee shop." Jerk.

He shrugged. "I wanted to be here on time."

"That's no excuse for being rude," I mumbled. And he hadn't even apologised.

"All right, everybody here for the graduate assessment centre, follow me." A loud voice carried over the reception and thirty of us stood and walked over to the medium built man in a dark suit. He waited a beat and I swear his eyes glowed white as he looked us over, his lips pursing the tiniest fraction as if unimpressed before leading us through the electronic gates into the building.

"Good luck," I whispered to Ariana as we got to our feet. I smoothed my suit again. No fear. Confidence. I got this.

Chapter 2

A business' building and its layout says a lot about the character of the place and the culture. Modern or traditional; staid or agile; comfortable or hungry. One ought to be able to get the impression of a company just by stepping foot inside its offices.

Elizabeth Bathory – *The First Disrupter*

The deeper into the building we got, the less modern it became, until we ended up in a plush basement lined with wooden panelling. My shoes ceased to clack as the tiles morphed into luxurious plain red carpet. We trailed after the man into a large room.

Oil paintings hung on golden strings attached to picture rails at the top of the high ceiling. One looked familiar and I read the nameplate: Elizabeth Bathory. I studied the painting. The woman staring back at me looked determined, even in her historic costume and with longer hair. There was nothing demure about her demeanour as she posed next to a lion. That was my idol. I reached out and touched the golden frame, trying to absorb some of her confidence and spirit through osmosis.

Four others in fitted suits that cost more than any of us wannabe graduates could afford shook our hands and introduced themselves before waving us into the leather swivel chairs set up around a large conference table.

"Thank you, Xavier," said the only woman in the room as we took our seats.

"It was my pleasure. New graduates afraid of their interviews taste the sweetest." The man who'd led us here licked his lips and smiled.

The woman shook her head and shooed him out. Once she had checked we were all seated, she clapped her hands. "Thank you all for coming today. I am Merissa Hope, Director of Human Resources and head of our graduate programme. Here at Bathory Corporation, we expect the best of the best, and today is designed to put you through your paces and select the best candidates. There will be group exercises and individual interviews, followed by presentations that you will have a chance to prepare during the lunch break. We will finish promptly at six o'clock." The woman rubbed her hands together. "In the interests of fairness, I should inform you that, this late in our selection process, we have only two spots left in the programme and I hope that two of you can fill those places as this is our last assessment centre of the year. If you are successful, we will inform you as soon as possible and you will start, with the rest of our graduates, on Monday. Are there any questions?"

A young man with the palest skin I'd ever seen raised his hand. "Where are the toilets?"

From her curled lip, I got the impression he'd already been marked down in her assessment, but she pointed the way, and he scampered off.

"OK, then," she smiled. "This half of the room will have their interviews first, if you can follow Mr Newton here, and the rest of you will have a group exercise to complete in this room."

I was in the interview group. I looked around and met the nervous gazes of the candidates next to me. We stood and filed out of the large room and back into the corridor, where Newton led us to individual interview rooms one by one. I was at the back of the line and he gave me a smile that showed his vampire teeth as he opened the final door and ushered me in. Something about him looked familiar…the rounded cheeks under the bags under his eyes and curly hair like something from a seventies rock band or the renaissance. Holy crap on a stick. Was that *Isaac Newton*? I sat a little straighter. I hadn't realised he was a vampire.

A young woman sat in one of the black leather swivel chairs. She stood, gave me a smile that didn't reach her eyes, and shook my hand before sitting back down. Newton edged around the low coffee table in the room and sat next to her, crossing his long legs before he gave me an appraising stare. He picked up a leather folder from the table and opened it, scanning something written inside.

"Miss Bruma, is it?"

I nodded and swallowed. There was a jug of water on the table and an empty glass in front of me. I leaned forward and poured myself some, ignoring the small drops that fell onto the polished surface of the table as I tipped the jug. The woman scribbled something in her notepad. Was that part of the interview? Had I messed up before I'd even started? I swallowed again. I had to treat this like a normal conversation. This was not public speaking, it was just three people talking.

"Please, call me Elle."

"This is Kylie, one of our current graduates. She'll be assisting me with this interview. Can you tell us why you're interested in working for the Bathory Corporation?"

I launched into my pre-prepared answer. Neither of their faces gave anything away. Newton glanced at the folder again.

"And you studied…mathematics at university?"

"Yes, with a minor in statistics. I enjoy the logic of numbers, the order they give us and the way they help us explain everything."

"What's your favourite statistic?"

My mind raced. What was I meant to say to that? My gaze lighted on the pen in his hand and I blurted out one of the stupid facts I had read. "On average, one hundred people die each year from ballpoint pens."

He raised an eyebrow. "Really? Fascinating."

The woman's mouth quirked up in a smile and she shot me

a pitying look. "And why are manhole covers round?"

The question threw me. We had moved into unchartered territory. I took a sip of my water while I puzzled it out. "So, they don't fall into the hole? If they were square or rectangular, then they could theoretically fall in if placed diagonally on their sides, but a round manhole cover that fits the space wouldn't ever fall in…"

"Are you telling us or asking us?" Newton asked.

"I don't know the answer," I admitted, "but that's my best estimate."

He nodded and wrote something down. My hands twitched, and I squashed the urge to smooth down my skirt again. I couldn't let the crazy out in an interview.

"Alright, now, what's the population of Birmingham?"

The questions followed a similar vein for the next ninety minutes. They alternated between asking questions about the value I could bring to the company with random questions that I worked my way through using logic.

"And where do you see yourself in five years?" Kylie asked.

"Ideally, I'd be in a role where I can add tangible value to the Bathory Corporation with responsibility for a team or department."

"Can you be any more specific?" Newton looked at me over steepled palms, his notebook on his lap.

"Based on my skills, I think I'd work well in an accounting or audit function."

"How about statistical modelling or underwriting?"

"Yes, those too. I modelled mathematical programmes for my final year project using General Pareto Distributions."

"And what would you do if you saw a colleague picking up a pound coin from the floor?"

I paused. "Did I see them drop it?"

"No."

"I think I'd assume it was theirs."

"But our company policy is to report any theft. If you can't be sure it's theirs, then it could be theft."

"I don't agree with stealing…but I wouldn't turn someone in for a pound."

Newton smiled, exposing small, pointed fangs. I squirmed like I was prey under his gaze. "Then, when would you report someone?"

We debated the numbers and other scenarios for a while and I almost got the sense he enjoyed our conversation when Kylie leaned forward and tapped her watch.

"Well, Miss Bruma, thank you very much for the interview, it's been very…insightful. Do you have any questions for us?"

I went through the usual questions about how I could expect to be challenged and what their policy was on qualifications before turning to Kylie.

"I'd love to know what you enjoy the most about the scheme."

She flicked her long blonde hair. "I didn't realise I was the one being interviewed." Her smile was hard and didn't meet her eyes. "But I really enjoy knowing that I'm the best I can be. Bathory Corporation is the elite. It's testing and I won't lie, it's tough, but I thrive in an environment like that and I know that I'm the best and everyone I work with is here because they're the best too. That's why it's so important that we make the right selection at these assessment centres…one rotten apple spoils the whole barrel and could besmirch the entire company."

Newton leaned forward. "Alright, thank you, Kylie." He stood.

I mirrored him, shaking both their hands again before following him back to the main room. I was shaken by the look Kylie had given me; I didn't fit into her idea of a good candidate. My hands balled into fists as I sat down, filled with the need to rearrange my suit.

The HR Director strode into the room after Ariana, who gave me a small smile and a wave. "Well, now, I hope you all had a lovely morning. We now have a short lunch break where we would like you to prepare a ten-minute presentation on your favourite thing to share with the whole group at the end of the day. At one p.m. those of you yet to be interviewed will be collected from here and the rest of you will have our group exercises. Ah, here's lunch, any dietary requirements you notified us of are written on the cards."

A man in a waistcoat and pressed grey trousers wheeled in a trolley piled with platters of sandwiches and fruit. He gave a small bow before leaving us alone.

There was a long pause, as if none of us wanted to be the first to get up before the arrogant graduate who was so confident he'd get a spot stood and strode over. "It's alright everyone; they're just sandwiches. They won't bite."

No one laughed at his poor joke, but we all got up. I was suddenly seized by the thought that my skirt had rumpled, and I looked a mess. Crap. The stress of the assessment was driving my thoughts into an uncontrolled frenzy.

I left them to it and raced to the bathroom, locking myself in a cubicle and allowing my compulsion free. I pressed my skirt seven times, then my jacket, then repeated it until I had done seven times seven. Extra lucky, and I needed every ounce of good fortune for the presentation later. My shoulders sagged with relief at getting out the tiny wrinkle and fulfilling my compulsion. Now, I just had to make it through the rest of the day.

Chapter 3

Teamwork is crucial to success. Anyone who says otherwise is lying. Without a committed team around one, there is a limit to what can be achieved. With a team, the possibilities are endless.

Elizabeth Bathory – *The First Disrupter*

I managed to eat a couple of the triangular sandwiches for lunch. There were only plain cheese and ham by the time I got back from the bathroom, but I forced two down and pulled out my notebook. It was a lucky notebook with a red leather cover embossed with tiny bat silhouettes. Maybe it was too cliché for a company run by vampires, but I'd saved it for everything Bathory. I skipped past the notes from my first round of interviews and tapped my pen on a blank page.

My favourite thing…I could talk about my best friend, Abby, but that felt too personal. Maybe my patchy hamster,

Nibbles. He was cute enough when he wasn't shedding and I found the way he packed away carrots funny, but somehow I didn't think a pet was the right tone for this group.

My other love was numbers, but what to choose? I drew a spiral on the table in a drop of condensation that had come from my glass. I blinked as I took in what my fingers had created. The Fibonacci sequence. Of course, the perfect thing.

I sketched it out on the page and wrote the numbers underneath, as many as I could remember. But that wasn't enough to fill ten minutes. Others had their smartphones out as they scribbled, so I dug mine out of my bag, pushing aside the Bathory autobiography, spare copies of my résumé and the chunky national record of achievement folder that I'd stuffed inside.

I looked up the Fibonacci sequence in nature – shells, flowers, pinecones – and popular culture – paintings, the Da Vinci Code, architecture, music. A list filled the page. That would be enough for ten minutes, especially if I explained what integers were and ended with why it illustrated the perfection of mathematics with the golden ratio that transcended knowledge so much that it had appeared in artwork for centuries. That sounded good and I wrote it down.

Too soon, the HR Director was back at the front of the room, splitting us into our two groups again. The interviewees – the group who had already completed the team tasks – gave us knowing smiles as they left and a few giggles erupted from the corridor, enough to send my stomach sinking to my feet.

"Now, we have a few exercises for you today, designed to

help us assess your teamworking skills, your logic, and your ability to stick to time. We'll start with something simple." She picked up a cardboard box from the side of the room and placed it on the table. "I'm going to split you into three teams of five and I want you to build the tallest tower from these materials." She upended the box and packets of spaghetti and marshmallows cascaded onto the polished wooden table.

"Aces," the tall bloke who'd been first in line for sandwiches said. I studied him to see if he was being sarcastic, but he looked genuine. *Who said 'aces'?* Someone who had been to a public school, knew how to tie a Windsor knot in his silk tie and had no problem barging into people in coffee queues, that's who. Pretentious prick.

"Mr Perron, I'm glad you're so excited about the task. You can be a team captain." With that, she divided us up and named captains for the other teams. My chest eased when she passed over me and picked someone else to lead. I wasn't ready for that responsibility.

What was the best way to build a tower? I ran through formulas in my head, but I hadn't studied engineering. I grabbed a packet of uncooked spaghetti and flexed a strand until it broke.

"What are you doing? Don't waste it!" Someone shouted.

"I wanted to test the tensile strength." I replied. "We need the tower tall, but also strong enough to stand."

"So, we should double up on the pasta, good thinking." The team leader snatched the packet out of my hand and began mashing strands into marshmallows.

"We should use triangles." I repeated myself three times to get heard in the rising noise of the room, but the team agreed and when the stopwatch went, we had a decent tower that supported itself. I risked a look at the other teams.

Perron's team had the tallest tower and gave themselves high fives as they beamed at everyone else. The third team's creation had collapsed and lay on the table in a sticky mess. I gulped and ignored my churning stomach. I couldn't be on the losing team and land my dream job. I needed to win.

The next task was a logic puzzle, and I sighed with relief.

"Can I see?" I said, grabbing at the single A4 sheet of paper.

Another team member plucked it from my hands. "No, Mr Green lives next to the yellow house, and that can't be blue because blue is between orange and red. It says here."

"If I could…" I noted the HR Director taking notes as she observed the team. They wanted assertive graduates. I took a deep breath. "Mr Green lives in the red house," I shouted over the din.

Four pairs of eyes looked my way. My palms heated and my skin flushed, but I wanted this job enough to push past my physical discomfort about speaking out. This was my last chance at a graduate scheme place. My ticket to success.

I held my hand out for the piece of paper. "It's simple logic. Here. Look." I picked up a pen and worked through the answers, explaining how I did it to the rest of the team, who nodded.

"Is it right that we just let her do it?" one asked, a tall woman with henna red hair.

"If she can do it the quickest, I say let her. A good team uses all its resources." The man who responded raised his voice on his last sentence and aimed it at the observers with a knowing smile. Creeping with the decision makers…I wish I'd thought of that.

I finished up the answers and pushed it across the table with a flourish. The HR Director didn't even bother to check the results, instead she jotted some more notes down and smiled at us.

"Well done, team two, you've finished first."

I took a small amount of pleasure as Perron's face turned a deep red of annoyance. He puffed out his cheeks and pulled his team's paper away from quiet Ariana before scribbling over her answers.

Merissa called time and finished her notes before giving us a final task.

"This will be your last team exercise, and this is for all of you. It's very simple, I want you to find the traitor." All fifteen of us eyed each other as she handed out slips of paper. "On these bits of paper, it says whether you are a traitor or not the traitor. Memorise them and hand them back to me, please." I unrolled my paper: Not a Traitor. A ripple of nervous laughter ran around the room as we handed them back in.

Perron leaned back with a smug smile on his pompous face. "This will be easy. I can read people like they're books."

"Well done, Mr Perron. Now, there is a tower in this box." The HR Director lifted a box onto the far end of the table with a smile. "I simply want you to match it exactly, using the bricks in this bag." She threw a blue drawstring bag at the nearest interviewee and he grunted as it hit him in the chest.

"The catch is that only one of you can look at the tower in this box at a time. You cannot speak while looking at the tower and then you cannot touch the bricks, only inform the others of their placement. You will each be allowed two trips to observe the tower for fifteen seconds per trip, and remember, there could be one or more traitors in your midst. You will have thirty minutes when I say go. Go."

There was a flurry of conversation around the best use of our time as the graduate who had the bag tipped the contents onto the table.

Perron strode to the box without consulting anyone and came back shouting out colours in an assertive voice that had everyone reaching for the blocks.

"Shouldn't we plan?" I tried. We had two looks each, that meant thirty opportunities to get this right, or twenty-eight if there was a traitor.

"We need to go for it," Perron replied, shooting me a look of disdain. "We've only got twenty seven minutes left."

"How many bricks were in the tower in total?" I asked.

"I didn't count. I got the bottom row for us, which Wayne is getting wrong. That green block goes first. You – go and look." He pointed to someone at random and the blonde scurried to the box and came back with a confused look on her face and called out some colours.

"What does that even mean? Are you the traitor?"

"No!"

This had descended into chaos quickly. I waved to get Merissa's attention. "Miss Hope, can I use both of my trips at the same time?" Ugh, I sounded like a schoolgirl, not a confident graduate.

She smiled like I had done something right. "Of course, but no more trips."

"OK, can I have quiet, please?" I asked.

The others sank back, mainly because they didn't have anything else to go on until someone went up. I kept my steps even, ignoring the thumping of my heart in my chest as they all stared at me. I nodded to the HR Director and looked in the box.

It was a simple tower. Twenty blocks in total. I memorised as much as I could, wishing I had an eidetic memory. But I didn't, so instead I went over the colours and sizes in my mind again and again until Merissa called time.

I ran back over, keeping my balance on my high heels, and pointed to one of the group. "First layer: green three by two block, red two by two block, yellow four by two block." I went through the second and third layer before my short-term memory failed. "That's all I know for sure."

"It was a green two block, not three by two."

"I know what I saw." I met Perron's gaze.

He fronted up to me. "Maybe you're the traitor."

"What would be the point of having a traitor in this exercise? We can fail well enough without anyone deliberately trying to mess it up." The logic didn't make sense. They wanted to test us, not pit us against each other.

"Spoken like a true traitor."

I clenched my fists. Fine. If he wanted to target me, I'd go on the attack. I wanted this too much to let him screw it up for me. "Or maybe the person who volunteered to go look first is the traitor. Classic move."

"I'm not a liar."

"You have twelve minutes left." Merissa's voice distracted us from the argument and there was a flurry of activity as the rest of the group lined up for their views before shouting out placements. All agreed that my initial three layers were right and I allowed a smug smile to curl my lips.

"And time. Well done everyone. Let's see how you did." The HR Director took the original tower out of the box. We didn't do too badly. "And now, will the traitors please reveal yourselves?" She looked around the room with a knowing smile.

"I was a traitor," Ariana stood.

"What? Impossible." Ms Hope's mouth fell open.

"I was," she insisted.

"The game is designed to sow mistrust among teams. There is no traitor, but the distrust remains. You must have read your paper incorrectly."

"Oh." She sank back into her chair. I gave her a small smile. This was a high-pressure environment and a split-second error might have cost her a chance at the spot. That might improve my odds, but I'd rather play fair.

"OK." The HR Director checked her schedule. "Now there is a ten-minute coffee break before your presentation. We'll go in alphabetical order."

My stomach jumped to my throat. The presentation. In the tangle of the team exercises, I'd almost forgotten about it. I ran to the toilet and splashed my face with water. I gripped the sink until my knuckles paled. It would be OK. I could do this. Last hurdle. If I wanted a job at the most prestigious company in the UK, I had to suck it up and get this done.

I met my pale brown eyes in the mirror and stifled a cry. The water had messed up my make-up. I grabbed paper towels and dabbed at my face, smearing mascara over my cheeks. I scrubbed again until my face was red, but the makeup smudges were gone. I swallowed. It was time to go back into the room.

The graduate scheme applicants crowded at the back of the room, squashed in their chairs as all the places at the table were filled with the Bathory employees who'd interviewed us. I couldn't find a seat so I stood next to an attractive man in a checked shirt; the only person not in a suit.

A balding man in a grey suit gave us a thumbs up and told us not to be nervous. His jacket was crumpled, unlike everyone else in their sharp suits. He'd make a good boss.

I wasn't first up. That was something. Ariana went through a presentation about the Cat Protection League. I saw Newton frown. Maybe he hated animals. It had been a good idea not to mention Nibbles.

But what if he hated my presentation, too? I couldn't present maths to one of the most important men in the history of science. What was I thinking? My legs dissolved into jelly.

Crap. This was bad. I couldn't faint in front of everyone. I must have made a noise because a youngish man with thick black glasses and a checked shirt offered me his seat. I sank into it.

"You look awful," he whispered as he poured me a glass of water. His lemony aftershave smelled fresh and summery, distracting me from the presentation I was about to give.

I took the water gratefully and made a non-committal noise.

"Nervous?" he asked. *Was it that obvious?* "Do you need something to distract yourself?" He pulled a keychain sized Rubik's cube from his pocket and handed it to me, his palm warm against my clammy skin.

I whispered my thanks and twisted the sides, regaining some semblance of calm. Puzzles I could do. I solved it, mixed it up and solved it again, not paying attention to the presentations going on at the other end of the room. Just breathe and solve the puzzle. I glanced up to see the kind man smiling down at me, one hand resting on the back of my chair. Crap. I'd taken his seat. But he didn't seem bothered.

Newton peered over at me from where he sat two seats down

the table, his head tilted to one side as he watched my hands move. I looked away.

The HR Director called my name. I took a breath and stood. My legs wobbled, and I clutched the tiny Rubik's cube so hard it cut into my palm. *It would be fine.* My logical brain tried to override my emotions, but each step felt like pushing against lead. I made it to the front and swallowed, gripping the pad with my notes in my hands. I stared at it, unable to make out my bullet points.

I looked up and the faces of everyone in the room swirled into blobs. A cough from the back drew my attention and I stared at Newton. His eyes glowed bright red as they met mine. There was a moment of calm as my brain lost all capacity to think.

"It's alright, Miss Bruma," Newton said, "take a breath and when you are ready, please continue."

I tried to force my lips up into a smile, but my face wouldn't cooperate. I opened my mouth like a goldfish and moved my lips once, twice, before my stomach cramped. I clamped my hand over my dry mouth and ran. Through my tears I saw him arch one eyebrow and write something down.

I sat panting on the cool floor of the toilet, my back against the hard door of the cubicle. I scrubbed a fleck of vomit off Abby's suit with a scrappy piece of toilet paper and sighed. She was going to kill me. I'd have to get it dry cleaned. I closed my eyes – how much did dry cleaning cost? Fifteen quid? Maybe thirty? There went my social budget for the week. And I'd blown the interview.

Chapter 4

Of course, I have had failures over the years, but the important thing is to learn from them, and have a strong group of people around you who can help you back to your feet. As I've said before; an individual is nothing without a strong team behind them. Sometimes, your biggest failures can turn into your best successes.

Elizabeth Bathory – *The First Disrupter*

One drink. That was how this mess had started. One little drink. I glared at my friend over the top of my glass. Or, I tried to. This was my fourth cocktail and things were fuzzy. Why had I agreed to drown my sorrows instead of curling up with Nibbles and the latest *Celebrity Baker*?

"I should go."

"You should stay," Abby countered.

I shook my head, tried to stand, and fell again. "This is your fault." I ruined the accusation with a squelchy burp at the end.

"You're displacing your feelings."

Sometimes it was so annoying being friends with an agony aunt.

"You're right. This is the Bathory Corporation's fault. Bloody vampires. One of them actually used 'besmirch' in a sentence."

"No."

I nodded and finished my drink.

"Then you don't need a place with those idiots, anyway." She raised her voice. "Besides, who even says vampires are real?"

I looked around and frowned. "Abby, we're in a vampire bar." That had been another one of her great suggestions; distract me from not getting a job at the vampire company by drinking at a bar run by them. The Bathory Corporation was a global conglomerate with fingers in all sorts of pies, including a chain of trendy bars.

"Fake," she said with a wink at me.

A male vampire appeared behind her. "We're not fake, see? All real." He flashed her a grin, showing his pointed fangs.

I tugged at Abby's dress under the table to get her to stop. *Don't wind up the vampires, Abby.*

She shrugged. "You can get fang implants."

"Why don't you come back to mine after work and I'll show you how real they are?" His voice was pure seduction over the sultry music in the cocktail bar.

Abby smiled, leaned forward, and whispered something in his ear that made his smile grow wider. He cleared our glasses and left us alone with a wink at her.

"Abby." I didn't like the whine in my voice, but I couldn't help it.

She lifted one shoulder. "What? I like supernaturals. They're so much…more."

"More what?"

"Everything," she purred.

I mimed throwing up, and she laughed.

"You OK making your own way home?"

I nodded and got up, using the chair to steady myself.

"And don't wallow, OK?"

"Wallow?" I repeated, sounding out the word. It sounded funny to my drunk ears so I said it again and once more because I could.

"I know you. This is their loss, not yours." She gave me a hug and sashayed into the crowd of patrons leaning against the copper plated bar.

I made my way to the taxi rank. All very well her saying not to dwell on things, but she hadn't been there. I had. Unfortunately, I had a front-row seat to my spectacular job interview failure.

The images ran through my mind as I pushed my way through the packed club. From the ill-fitting suit that I was still wearing to my spectacular exit at the end. The worst had been the sympathy in Newton's eyes when I crept back into the room at half past six, when I was sure everyone would have left.

Only Newton and the guy in the checked shirt had been there and both had given me twin looks of condescending compassion before I'd grabbed my bag and fled, my cheeks burning. I'd only realised later that I'd stolen the handsome younger man's Rubik's cube.

I groaned aloud and rubbed my face, as if that could make the memories of failing in front of Isaac Newton – mathematical genius – disappear. Newton, for goodness' sake. *Why couldn't it have been anyone but him?* I crashed into something solid and opened my eyes, feeling my cheek rubbing against thick material.

"Miss Bruma? How are you feeling?" *Oh no.* I recognised that voice. As if my thoughts had conjured him, the curly-haired vampire stood in front of me, arms around me.

"Better," I mumbled into his plush, woollen coat, pushing myself back a step. I wanted to get away from anything to do with that nightmare interview, including my mathematical hero.

"That was one of the most interesting assessment centres I have had the pleasure of attending in a long time."

"I'm glad I could make it entertaining for you," I snapped, before clamping my lips together. He was being nice. It was my own fault I'd messed this up. Who couldn't even run through a presentation on their favourite topic? Me. That's who.

The right-hand corner of his mouth quirked up.

"I'd better go." I turned to leave and muttered, "Bloody vampires," under my breath. His hand shot out and gripped my upper arm like a vice.

"Is that any way to speak about your employers?"

"What?" I stared stupidly at him.

"Congratulations, Miss Bruma, you have a place on Bathory Corporation's graduate scheme, should you choose to accept it…and I strongly suggest that you do."

My mouth gaped open, and my heart flew. "Really?"

"You will receive the official call in the morning along with the required paperwork, but, as we bumped into each other – literally – it seemed right to tell you now…before you do anything foolish."

"Why?" I clamped a hand over my mouth. "I mean, thank you…but, why?"

"Despite your…issue with the presentation, you had a strong interview and demonstrated good thinking in the group exercises and your trick with the cube was most impressive. We felt that outweighed the development areas you clearly have. I look forward to seeing you on Monday, Miss Bruma." He looked me up and down. "Do you need assistance getting home?"

"No," I blurted out. "I don't normally…I mean, this isn't…"

He chuckled, a deep sound that made me feel like a little kid. "Don't worry, I make it a point not to concern myself what our graduates do with their free time. Enjoy it now. You won't get much when you start work. If you'll excuse me." Newton released me and strode to the bar where he found a spot and got the attention of the bartender without much more than a curl of his lip. I tottered to the door and glanced back before heading into the cool night air. Newton watched me from the bar and raised his glass in my direction. A shiver snaked down my spine and I had the sudden thought that I was prey caught in a trap.

I shook off my discomfort, held my head high, and marched out to get a taxi back home. As the cold air hit me and sobered me up, his words reverberated through my mind. I had a job. With the Bathory Corporation. A stupid grin grew across my face, and I did a fist pump, causing a group of barely dressed ladies out on a hen do – complete with novelty penises on their headbands – to give me a wide berth on the pavement. Their headbands wobbled wildly as they moved out of my way.

The smile stayed on my face all the way back to our shared flat where I fed Nibbles his hamster treats, undressed and collapsed on my single bed. "I got the job, Nibbles."

He squeaked in reply and devoured the treats, shoving them all into his cheek pouches in one go until his chubby face was all distorted. Yeah, he was excited for me. I could tell.

Chapter 5

Dear Abby, What advice do you have for someone starting a new job? I'm really nervous.

Honey, congratulations on your new job! Now let's thought cake this problem. I get you might be nervous (that's the icing layer in our thought cake). Just remember; no one expects you to be perfect on your first day, so just pay attention, smile, don't be afraid to ask lots of questions, and take notes – it shows you're keen. No one's going to fire you on your first day (I expect that's your first layer of this cake thought). You've worked hard to get here, and they want you, so you're starting from a position of strength and believe me, they did not make a mistake hiring you (did I just get to the gooey centre of this thought cake and the real reason you're nervous?). Everyone wants you to succeed.

But it never hurts to bring in some sweet treats for the team on your first day.

Yours cakefully, Abby

Abby Wright – *Ask Abby*

I hung at the top of the zipwire, staring out over the treetops, muttering to myself. "Come on, it's not that big."

Tristan Perron – the overconfident prick from the assessment centre – grinned at me from his spot next to mine. "That's what she said." He held out his hand for a high five. No one returned it. He launched himself off the other line with a shout of "Get on with it!" before whooping with joy as he skimmed the treeline and disappeared into the greenery.

"Don't listen to him," a tall, green-skinned orc said as an instructor strapped her into a harness. "I hate heights too."

I shot her a look of thanks.

"Let's do it together."

I nodded. I hadn't got through the nightmare assessment centre and crawled through mud during this graduate team build to give up at the top of a cliff edge. If throwing myself off the edge was what the Bathory Corporation wanted, then I would throw myself into the unknown. I'd taken some lavender tablets that Abby promised would calm my nerves and told my obsessive thoughts to go suck it. Besides, my brain was so shocked at the thought of throwing myself off this cliff that it couldn't even think up a compulsion to counteract this insanity.

"Just, what's the injury rate?" I asked. "Per hundred?"

The instructor laughed at my question. "Haven't lost anyone on a graduate scheme yet."

That was reassuring. Not.

"OK, on the count of three," he said. "One."

"Two," the orc said.

I took a breath. It could be worse; it could be public speaking.

"Three!" I yelled, launching myself off the swaying platform and into the air. The harness snapped tight. I clamped my mouth shut as I hurtled over the trees so fast I could no longer see the leaves, only a blur of green. My stomach felt like I'd left it back on the platform and the wind rushed past my ears, freezing my exposed skin. I was free, flying across the forest. Was this what birds felt like? It was awful.

And then it was over. My legs hit the ground with a bump, my stomach caught up with my body, but I wasn't sick. My body buzzed with adrenaline and my eyes were bright as the instructor at this end of the wire unclipped my harness. I laughed. I'd freaking made it and yes, I patted myself up and down, still alive.

"Well done," she said before turning to unstrap the orc.

I walked over and shook her huge green hand.

"You did it," she smiled at me, exposing her pointed lower teeth.

"So did you." I paused. I had forgotten her name. I decided to play it cool. "I'm Elle."

"Precious Sturmrock. Nice to meet you. Crazy place." She jerked her head to the sprawling country house that sat behind the assault course we'd just finished. It was our home for the three days we were on this course, and it was indeed a bit crazy to eat breakfast in a grand dining room. I'd sent Abby a ton of photos and she'd told me to enjoy living in a Regency drama.

"Yeah. It's a bit much, but I guess it's meant to bond us as a team."

She shrugged and turned her head towards the group still high five-ing by the base of a large pine tree. "Some of us are bonding more than others."

I nodded. They were like a frat house or something. I could never understand how people could make friends that quickly, but I'd done some reading and had prepared some small talk.

"So where are you from?"

"Camden. There's a big orc community there. I love it, but it's not somewhere you stay if you want to make something of yourself."

"I'm from all over. Foster system." That was enough said about that. "I'm moving to London in a couple of weeks."

"That's cool. I can't wait to get my own place, but I'm saving up first, so I'm living with Mum and Dad for a while."

"Sounds cosy."

"Too cosy with five older brothers."

"Wow, that's a big family."

"Too big sometimes. Come on, we'd better go. Looks like we're done for the day."

The instructor wrapped up by making us all stand in a circle and put our hands in the centre before shouting "Teamwork" as loud as we could. I couldn't help my smile as we yelled. These were my people. We would be together for the next eighteen months and more in the company, assuming we survived the Reaping at Christmas. A spark of hope ignited deep in my chest that these colleagues would become a family of sorts.

We raced back to the enormous gothic revival country house to change for the final dinner. I was tired and sore from all the outdoor exercises, but I was happy. I stepped into the ensuite shower in my room and scrubbed off the mud from today's assault course in the steaming water.

Back in the plush bedroom – the Bathory Corporation didn't skimp on hotel rooms – I got changed into my trusty grey suit. It was the only formal wear I had brought, the only formal wear I owned, and I wanted to impress. The rumour was that Elizabeth Bathory herself attended the final night dinner.

I checked my reflection and lifted my dark hair into a tight bun. It was so black it was almost purple in the hotel room light. I brushed on some mascara and debated covering up my birthmark, but decided against it, instead I pulled a couple of tendrils of hair and let them fall over the black mark by my ear. I took a deep breath, grabbed my handbag, and turned off the lights. Then switched them on again. Seven times. My lucky number. That would make sure tonight went well.

In the hallway, I locked my room. Seven times.

"Hey, let's go down together."

I turned to see Precious bouncing down the hall in a tight

dress that hugged her curves, her long legs accentuated by heels that added four inches to her tall frame.

"Wow, I love your earrings."

The bright red acrylic hoops hung from her lobes, daring the world to look at her. She shook her head, and the loops swung in time with her movements. She laughed – a throaty sound that made me long for shared jokes with a family more than I had in a long while. "Don't fit in when you can stand out." She said it like it was a statement.

"Yeah." My laugh was weaker, and I smoothed down my grey suit jacket. All I wanted was to fit in, get ahead, prove I was worth something. I wished I had the confidence to wear colourful jewellery or not care about what others thought, but that was a luxury that would have to wait until I was head of a department…or a director.

She linked her arm through mine, and we headed downstairs to the dining room.

For the formal dinner, the enormous table was laid with white china, many different rows of shining cutlery and candles shone in tall candelabras that softened the atmosphere. The graduates clustered around a smaller table where a man in a tailored waistcoat handed out drinks.

Precious steered us over and grabbed two flutes of champagne. I sipped and looked around. There were thirty-seven place settings, but only twenty of us on the graduate scheme.

"Do you think she's really coming?" I asked. "Bathory, I

mean?"

"No idea." She shrugged and drank up. I sipped the champagne and the small bubbles trickled down my throat like silk. This was expensive stuff. Or so I heard one of the others say. Foster homes weren't exactly the best place to learn about fancy wines.

"Hey, waiter," Tristan said by my ear, "any chance of some more canapés?"

I looked around, but Tristan's comment was aimed at me.

"I'm not a waiter." I stared at him, but he just blinked at me. "I'm on the graduate programme with you. We were on the same assessment centre. We've spent three days together on this course."

He squinted at me for a second before recognition dawned. "Vomiticious! Crazy. Guess they scraped the bottom of the barrel to get you here." He turned to his mates. "This one threw up. At the assessment centre!" Some of them laughed. I wished the floor would swallow me. "Sorry I didn't recognise you. I mean," he waved his hand at me, "the suit, and you weren't running out of the room to throw up." He held up a hand for a high five from one of his cronies and wasn't disappointed.

My cheeks heated, and my stomach swirled. I tightened my grip on the champagne, determined not to run off.

"Leave her alone." Precious stepped in while my mind still raced, searching for a response.

"Who are you again?" Tristan leered at her.

"Precious."

He snorted out a laugh. "Sounds like a dog's name." He started barking and a couple of others joined in.

Precious handed me her glass and squared up to him. She easily matched his six-foot something height and looked him straight in the eye. Her fist clenched. "Say that again, pretty boy."

He placed a hand on her arm. She sidestepped and twisted it up his back. "Touch me again and I'll rip your arm off."

The door opened, and in swept Elizabeth Bathory, flanked by sixteen others.

Chapter 6

First impressions are everything. The second you enter a room, everyone should know that you are the most powerful and most dangerous person in there. Only after that, will anyone take you seriously.

Elizabeth Bathory – *The First Disrupter*

Precious released Tristan, shoving him away from us as we watched Elizabeth Bathory enter.

The CEO and Chairwoman of the Bathory Corporation was everything I expected and more. Her slick bob framed her angular jaw, and an elegant black dress draped her body with an air of sophistication that spoke of old money. She halted inside the doors and waited for every gaze to turn towards her before she lifted her lips in a smile that showed her pristine white pointed teeth and raised her hands.

"Thank you for waiting." I checked my watch – she was punctual. "Please, let us sit."

Looks like there wouldn't be an opportunity for mingling. I made my way to the table, a small frown creasing my forehead as I realised that Tristan Perron had bagged a seat to her right. He leant over to say something, but she turned the other way and spoke to the woman on her left. I hid my smile and sat down next to Precious.

Once we all had seats, Elizabeth Bathory stood and touched a spoon to her glass, sending a high-pitched ringing over the table. We turned to look. She waited a second, gathering our attention to her like she was born to the limelight.

"These aren't real silver," Precious whispered, inspecting her fork.

I gave her a questioning look.

"Vampires can't touch silver." She shrugged at my raised eyebrow. "My brothers made me learn every single piece of vampire lore when I got the job."

"Welcome to the Bathory Corporation, and congratulations," Elizabeth Bathory said. "Merissa," the HR Director inclined her head at the mention of her name, "tells me that we had over two thousand applicants and you are the top twenty. You should be proud of yourselves." She clapped her hands together, and the others joined in. I glanced around the table and clapped too, desperate to fit in.

Tristan let out a whoop and a couple of the others copied him. Elizabeth smiled, but the humour didn't reach her eyes. She stopped suddenly, lapsing into preternatural stillness. The applause died out as quickly as it had begun, leaving a few of the graduates clapping in the sudden silence of the hall before they stopped out of embarrassment.

"I want to reassure you that you have made the right choice joining us here at the Bathory Corporation, which is why I am proud to call you family with all the privileges and obligations that entails. This is the start of your journey with us and, if you excel, you will have a prosperous career with the company. We have the best of the best working at my company – the elite, if you will. And your mentors and buddies from the previous year's intake will guide you through your new life at our corporation."

The people who'd walked in with her nodded to us and I repressed a shudder. The younger ones must be the graduates from last year, and they all looked like they'd happily watch us crash and burn. The older ones were the mentors and most of them stared at their glasses, disinterested in their CEO's speech, but Newton's eyes burned into mine like I was a calculus problem he wanted to solve. I swallowed. *Please don't let me have him as a mentor.*

"We are known throughout Europe as the premiere company for audits and advice and have several subsidiaries where you will be able to prove that we made the right decision in hiring you and I look forward to seeing you thrive. But, a word of warning. The path of progression is not easy and your place here is not guaranteed." Her gaze landed on each of our faces as she spoke. I squirmed in my seat, tapping my heel against the chair.

"Through the course of your placements, your managers and

mentors and any of your colleagues will be asked to provide assessments of you and, of course, you will be expected to complete your professional qualifications as well."

I nodded along. All as expected so far.

"There will be a selection ceremony after your first placement to decide if you have achieved our exacting standards." That wasn't in the glossy information packs they'd sent me.

"What happens if we fail?" asked one of the graduates; an innocent-looking young man named Sunil.

"If you are judged not up to standard, your contract will be terminated." She paused and inclined her head as she raised her glass. "To our new graduates."

A murmur rang around the room as we returned the toast, much of the low conversation laced with shock at the cold delivery of the announcement that we could be unemployed by Christmas. Bathory sat, ignoring the chatter, and the food was served. A waitress placed a steaming bowl of soup in front of me and another offered me a bread roll. I took one and waited for someone else to start before I copied them, selecting the same spoon from the rows of cutlery as Precious did. I didn't want to make a faux pas in front of the CEO and it wasn't like they taught etiquette at state schools.

"What did you think of that speech?" I asked Precious as I buttered my poppy seed roll.

Precious shrugged and took a spoonful of the brown soup. "Simple enough. Make sure you do well, or you'll be sacked."

"It's not an idle threat." A tenor voice interrupted us, and I looked up into the bright eyes of a balding man that I recognised from the assessment centre.

"We call it the Reaping." The blonde who'd interviewed me grinned at us with the confidence that came from knowing their job was secure.

"The selection ceremony happens at the end of your first placement. It's designed to make sure you're a good fit for the company, that's all," said the bald man. "There's a fifty per cent dropout rate in the first twelve months, and half of that is at the selection ceremony. I hope you'll both make it, though." He raised his glass to us before taking a sip of the red liquid. I stared at his mouth, unable to help myself. He laughed and tapped his teeth. "Albert Ahrenns. I'm human. One of few directors who aren't vamps, but you'll get the lay of the land soon enough." He chuckled and downed his wine.

I swallowed. "What about you?" I asked the older graduate seated to my other side.

"Kylie Cartan. HR and trained accountant."

"When you pass your exams," Albert chimed in.

She shot him a look that should have speared him to his chair. "I hope you're up to our standards. I'd hate to see the Bathory Corporation weakened by a bad batch; it only takes a few rotten apples to poison the whole bunch." She'd said the same thing at the assessment centre. Maybe it was the only saying she knew.

"Do you know who you're buddied with?" I asked, moving

us away from bad fruit similes. Or metaphors. English wasn't my strong suit; I was more at home with maths and sciences.

Kylie lifted one shoulder, causing her off-the-shoulder dress to ripple. "We find out on Monday."

"And you look after us?"

She laughed. "In a way."

I shared a look with Precious, who shrugged. It was too late to back out now, but I got the feeling that if this company was a family, it was the sort with a lot of skeletons buried under the lawn.

"Do you know who the mentors are paired up with?"

"Why? Are you eyeing up Newton?" Kylie laughed. "The new ones always like him."

"What? No." My face heated, and I cursed my stupid shyness. Now it looked like I did have a crush on the ancient mathematician. I focused on the white tablecloth, trying to calm the blood away from my face.

"Why not? He's alright to look at, if you like the whole academic vibe."

"And he's got such good hearing, too," Newton said, smiling towards us.

Unflustered, Kylie returned his grin. "Just having a joke with the newbies." He raised one eyebrow, and she shifted in her seat. "Sir," she said behind her false smile.

"Good. Humour is important in the workplace." He turned away.

I covered my snort of laughter into a cough as the main course arrived.

Chapter 7

Some people think I am against new technology. Nothing could be further from the truth. Technology is necessary for progress.

Elizabeth Bathory – *The First Disrupter*

I stared at my pass as I waited in another vast conference room in the deep basement of the Bathory Corporation's London headquarters. The picture was unflattering, washing out my pale skin and the tight bun made me look like I had no hair, but the dark Bathory logo of a bat in the centre of a shield drew the eye so maybe it didn't matter.

Tristan was in the seat next to me, his legs sprawled out. "Show me yours and I'll show you mine." He threw his pass onto the table and I couldn't resist glancing at his photo. He looked like a model for a preppy catalogue. I shook my head, but I placed my own piece of plastic next to his in a peace offering. Maybe, underneath his obnoxious personality, we could be friends. He picked it up and squinted at my picture, then at me.

"Not very photogenic, are you? The camera loves me, I once filled in for a shoot in Vogue. Shame about the dirt. Didn't you wash this morning?" He handed it back and studied my face. "Yeah, you missed a bit." Tristan leaned forward to brush the dirt off my reddening face. I held still, hating his touch, but not knowing how to respond. He rubbed a spot by my ear, then frowned. "Huh, won't come off."

I put my hand up to my face to stop his attempts to clean me up. "It's a birthmark," I said, realising too late what he'd spotted.

"Oh, right." He looked a tiny bit uncomfortable before his confidence caught up. "Sorry, looked like a speck."

I pulled a strand of hair out of my bun and over the dark mark by my ear.

"Don't listen to him, he's a prick," Precious said from her spot next to me. Today her earrings were red triangles that matched her bright suit dress and jacket. She glared at him.

"I won't." I swallowed. "It's not his fault he only looks good in photographs."

She howled a laugh. "Yass!" She fist bumped me with her large hand and grinned over my head at the obnoxious human.

He puffed up his chest and opened his mouth, but the HR Director entered, preventing whatever nastiness he was plotting.

"Welcome to our new graduates! The hard work starts now.

These folders contain floor plans, useful information, acceptable professional qualifications and the names of your buddy and mentor. I will be the primary contact for the graduate scheme, and, if you have any questions or problems, I expect you to come to me. My door is always open. To help you with your first day, we have a small goody bag for you."

I took the folder and black paper bag she handed me. I swallowed as I saw the name of my mentor peeking out of the folder. Newton. Figured. The short paragraph about him noted he was a Special Advisor to the company – whatever that meant – as well as holding several degrees and so many letters after his name that he could win a game of scrabble. With a sigh, my gaze drifted to the buddy I'd been assigned.

There was a full CV and a name: Kylie Cartan. The name rang a bell, but I'd met so many people at the dinner last week, I couldn't remember what she looked like. At least she was training to be an accountant so I could ask her about that qualification. Ordering numbers into neat rows appealed to me and felt like it was something I could control, unlike the rest of my life.

I looked at my assignment for the first placement: Audit (Fae). Inside, I groaned. I didn't have a passport. It took me a microsecond to decide not to say anything or ask for an alternative placement. I needed to fit in here and do well if I wanted to make it to director level in five years. Besides, how long did it take to get a passport? Surely I could fast track it.

"What did you get?" I whispered to Precious.

"Fae Audits."

"Me too."

"And me." I twisted round to see smug Tristan looking our way. "Looks like we'll be audit buddies." I didn't like the way his lips curved up.

Next to the folder was a sleek, black laptop and the goody bag. I pulled out a brown moleskin notebook and pen, a warm feeling spreading through my chest as I saw my name engraved in the pen with swirling writing. I belonged here. I sat up a little straighter, some of the uneasy feeling in my chest unwinding.

"OK, now that you've all got your assignments, let's test your laptops." Merissa watched as we all turned them on. She guided everyone through their logons.

I raised my hand. "My laptop isn't turning on."

She narrowed her eyes at me and strode over, tapping the on button with force before she conceded that I was right. She clapped her hands together. "Looks like you'll get to meet our IT department. Take it up to Basement One. The rest of you can meet your buddies in the canteen for coffee and pastries before they take you up to your departments. Have a wonderful first day of the rest of your career."

With that, the HR Director led the way out of the room and back along the corridor to the lift. I piled in with the first group and pressed the button for B1. The meeting rooms were on B2, but there was a B3 as well.

"What's on B3?" I asked.

"The Archives," Merissa replied, pronouncing the capital

letter. "But you won't need to worry about that."

My stomach flipped as the elevator came to a halt. The doors parted with a ping and she looked at me expectantly until I got out. The others carried on to the ground floor. This corridor was grey and dull compared to the opulence of the lower basement that housed the meeting rooms. It looked like the sort of place where someone was murdered, and they never found the body.

I clutched the laptop to my chest with one arm and crept forwards, wincing as my heels clacked on the grey floor. If anyone was looking for a murder victim, they could just follow the tap tap of my shoes.

There was only one direction to go, so I hurried along, shifting my weight to my tiptoes to dampen the clicking noise of my heels. I paused in front of a set of heavy-duty doors in a darker shade of grey to the corridor. There was no sign on them. I squinted through the thin panel of glass in the left-hand door.

"Hello?"

I jumped at the voice behind me and spun round. My paper bag with the notebook hit my would-be assailant.

"Ouch."

I took in the checked shirt, corduroy trousers and the pass that hung around his neck before dragging up my gaze to a handsome face framed by dark hair and a pair of square glasses that made his eyes look intense. He looked familiar. He waited for me to say something. I licked my lips. "Sorry."

"No problem. I often get attacked on my way into work." He smiled as he said it. A joke?

"Really?"

"No." He thought for a moment. "Not by a bag anyway." He flashed me a smile.

I frowned, unsure what to make of his statement. I decided to get to the point. "Merissa Hope, the HR Director sent me here. My laptop's not working." I held out the offending item as proof of my statement.

He gave a sigh and held his pass up to a small sensor. The door released with a click, and he pushed it open. Once inside, he sank into a swivel chair next to a long table that held laptops and other computer paraphernalia in various states of assembly.

"Hand it over then."

I scurried over to his desk and placed the laptop down on the veneered surface. The room was lined with metal racking that held more IT equipment. Under the fluorescent light, they gleamed like strange dormant insects waiting for a command to attack. There were no windows.

He tapped at the keyboard. While he worked, I studied him. He had high cheekbones, long thick lashes – it was unfair how men got those while mine were clumpy and a small scar above his lip that made his handsomeness more accessible. When he spoke, I jumped and looked away before he could catch me staring. "They've given you a duff battery. I'll replace it."

"Don't the laptops come from your department?"

He gave me a look and dug through a pile of keyboards until he found a small screwdriver. "How long have you worked here?" he asked.

"First day."

He stopped and looked me up and down. "Air of optimism and keenness, still got some colour to you." He leaned back and levelled his screwdriver at me. "I bet you're one of the new graduates."

I frowned. "What does that mean?"

"Just that the longer you work here, the more they take from you. Right down to your youthful glow."

"How long have you worked here, then?" He had a wan tinge to his skin. Maybe from working here, maybe from being hidden in the IT department.

"Five years in March."

"Why stay if you hate it?"

"I can't leave." He said it with an intensity that stilled my tongue on a reply about IT skills being transferable.

We looked at each other for a long moment, both struggling to understand what we meant. I broke our gaze first and my eyes lit on a row of different puzzle boxes lined the desk, tucked neatly against the wall. I thought he looked familiar; he'd given me the Rubik's cube keyring at the assessment centre.

While he pressed buttons, I dug around in my bag until my fingers closed on the cube. "I think this is yours."

He stopped working and leaned back, assessing me. "Did it help?"

"More than you know." It didn't stop me throwing up, though. I blushed. He probably remembered me as the idiot who was sick at her assessment centre.

"Keep it."

"I couldn't–"

"It's a keyring, not a diamond ring. Keep it."

"OK." I closed my hand around the cube. "Thank you."

He grunted and went back to the laptop.

"Do you know how long it'll take?" I broke the silence.

"Got somewhere you need to be?"

"Yes, actually. I should be upstairs meeting my buddy, then my new manager."

"Important day."

"Yes." This conversation was stressing me out. I should be somewhere else. Even now, they might decide to rip away the job they'd given me, realise it had all been a mistake. I inhaled deeply in a vain attempt to calm the thoughts that whirled around my head. I could feel the compulsion coming and I tightened my grip on the paper bag handle, feeling the string cut into my palm.

He flicked the old battery out and replaced it with a twirl of the screwdriver. "All done. Wouldn't want to keep you waiting."

"Thank you…"

"Liam." He stood and gave a mock bow. "IT expert at your service. Come see me for all your IT needs."

A ping sounded down the hall, and he jumped up.

"Really? Thank–"

He thrust the laptop into my arms. "Go on. Get back upstairs to your party."

He ushered me out and I stood gaping in the life sucking hallway before heading back to the elevator. That was rude. A thin man in a cardigan passed me in the corridor.

"Well, hello, and who might you be?"

Before I could answer, Liam stuck his head out of the IT room. "Greg, there's a load of refurbs here with your name on it. Snack later."

Greg's lips twitched, but he passed by and left me to it. I scampered to the lift and got in, jamming my thumb against the Ground Floor button until the doors closed, and I was left alone. That was weird. Anger flushed through my chest. And rude. I checked my watch and inhaled deeply seven times. The elevator came to that stomach-lurching stop, and I hurried through the atrium to the canteen.

Chapter 8

Initially, I founded the Bathory Corporation as a refuge for others like me. There has not always been as much tolerance for supernaturals as there is now. This has led to the corporation winning many awards for equal employment and I'm proud to say that mundane humans and magical beings work together for the greater good of the company.

Elizabeth Bathory – *The First Disrupter*

"You're late." The first words out of my buddy's mouth. She was tall and blonde with a slim frame covered by a well-fitted suit. My heart sank as I recognised her from dinner.

"Sorry, I–"

She held up a hand. "I don't care. Come on." She strode back to the elevator and got inside, tapping her foot as she waited for me to join her.

"I'm Noelle, but everyone calls me Elle."

She grunted. "I can read a file."

I searched for a name, couldn't remember it and scrabbled through my folder. The papers fell to the floor. She leaned back against the elevator panelling and watched as I scrambled to pick everything up.

"Thanks for the help," I found a name amongst the sheets of A4, "Kylie."

She folded her arms. "It's not my job to babysit you."

"I thought we were buddies."

"We have a professional relationship dictated by corporate graduate policy. Officially, I'm here to guide you and introduce you to the Bathory Corporation's way of working. But, let me be clear. I do not want any distraction from you. This place is cutthroat enough as it is and I don't need any whining about your pathetic problems."

"So, what then?"

"We will meet once a month and I will sign your progress book. If you contact me outside of those times for anything that is not work-related, I will mark you down on your assessments. Clear?"

I nodded. "As crystal."

The doors opened, and she strode ahead to the Fae Audits department. I swallowed and followed after her. This was not what I'd expected from my first day. Maybe my hopes had been too high, but all thought of proving myself and making friends, maybe even having drinks after a hard day in the office was rapidly fading away as the reality of corporate life hit me.

Inside the double doors to the department, Tristan slumped at his desk. Precious held her hand to her neck, looking like she wanted to punch someone.

I opened my mouth to ask what was wrong when a vampire slammed into me and shoved me against the wall. I cried out as he sank his teeth into my neck and drank deeply. My heartbeat pounded in my ears and I struggled against his weight, but he had my arms pinned. I felt myself weakening. I was going to die on my first day at the job and no one stepped forward to help me. My gaze searched the room for aid, but all I could focus on was Kylie's smug smile as she folded her arms and watched my attacker drain me. After a last drink, the vampire pushed me away.

"Ugh, what are you?"

I wiped my wound and stared at the crimson blood on my fingers. I'd been bitten. It took me a moment to take it in.

"You have to say on your pass if you've got any diseases. Or if you're supernatural. I should know what I'm eating."

"I don't have any diseases." Not that I knew of.

"Well, you taste disgusting." He screwed up his nose. "You're not a banshee, are you?"

"Now, now, Fred, leave our graduates alone." It was the kind gentleman from the meal, Albert someone. He offered me a yellow plaster for my neck. "Sorry about that, Noelle, but our senior managers get excited for new blood."

I gaped up at him. Oh crap. Did this mean I was a vampire now? Could I get any diseases from him? Mouths were full of bacteria. This was bad. Bile filled my throat.

"Company policy. It was in the paperwork you signed." Albert's round face showed concern as if it was his fault I hadn't read the fine print. "Any vampire at senior manager level or above can help themselves to junior employees, to a limit of once per week and no more than half a pint of blood. The plaster – and the lanyard – makes sure everyone knows you've been tapped this week. Turn your pass around."

OK, I could do that. It helped to have instructions.

Albert waited until I'd flipped it so the lanyard showed the yellow side instead of the navy blue. "There. Think of it as an initiation. Most of them use the blood bank for donations, but they get a bit carried away with the new graduates. Of course, you don't have to worry about that from me." He smiled, showing his human teeth, and rubbed his hands together. "Albert, Director of Fae Audits and your manager for this placement. That's your desk over there. Thank you, Kylie, you can go."

"Enjoy your first day and remember to let me know if you need anything." My buddy's smile didn't meet her eyes, and I knew that look meant that if I dared to email her, she'd give me a negative assessment so fast, I might as well hand in my laptop and badge today. I smiled back – more of a grimace than a grin – and my shoulders sagged with relief when she left. I just had to put a brave face on, and I'd been doing that for most of my life so a few more hours until I could look up how people got turned into vampires was fine.

Precious gave me a small wave from her seat, and I noticed

the same bright yellow plaster on her neck. So that was why she hadn't come to my aid. But why hadn't she fought off the vampire? She was pushing six feet without heels and looked like she could fit in on any rugby team.

"Damn vamps are too fast, but it won't happen again," she muttered as I took a seat at the desk next to her.

"Right, well, it's a nice easy day for you graduates today," Albert said with a bright grin. "Corporate induction. Unfortunately, our training system is down, but luckily we don't throw anything away. I found some DVDs in the cupboard and I've booked out our meeting room so you can watch the videos in there. Should take you all day. Oh, and let me introduce you to Debbie. She's our assistant and she'll help out with anything you need."

Debbie gave us a bright smile. "Let me know if you need anything at all. I'm always happy to help. Here's your training videos." She dumped a stack of DVD cases into our arms and pointed to a room in the corner of the office.

We tromped into the meeting room – less plush than the ones in the basement – and I folded myself onto an ergonomically designed grey chair that was the most uncomfortable thing I'd ever sat on. Debbie fumbled with the connector for a while.

"I suggest you start with this one." Debbie held up a case that read *'So you've been bitten by a colleague'*.

I felt a yawn creeping up on me as she fiddled with the TV. The assistant managed to plug the cable in and then flicked through every single input on the TV. Twice. By the time

Debbie had loaded in the first DVD, we were all slumping in our seats.

Debbie grinned at us, her eyes glowing slightly, although that might have been my imagination in the stuffy room. "I'll leave you to it. Thanks for your patience."

The DVD started with the facts that vampires were allowed to feed on junior employees and this didn't turn anyone into a vampire as it required a longer process and blood sharing to transmit the vampire virus. *Thank goodness.* I sighed a breath of relief; turning into a vampire was one less thing to worry about.

But what about diseases? The DVD had that covered too; vampires didn't get the same diseases as humans, so they weren't transferred during feeding. Another piece of tension eased off my chest. I'd still look it up later, but this had given me some reassurance.

As the smiling man talked us through the fact that not all vampires were members of nobility and didn't live in castles and it was stereotyping to even bring it up, I recovered my spirits and turned to Precious. "This is not how I thought the first day would be."

"What did you expect, Speckle?" Tristan cut across me. "Sunshine and raindrops? Welcome to the corporate world, kid."

I frowned at Tristan. "I wasn't talking to you. And Speckle?"

"I thought it was better than Vomiticious. You know, cos of

your mark." He pointed at my face, and I brushed my hair over my ear to cover the birthmark. "But we can go back to Vomiticious if you like?"

"It's not even that big."

"That's what she said," he smirked.

I rolled my eyes at his poor joke. "What's your nickname, then?"

"Stud."

I blurted out a laugh.

He shrugged. "I can't help what people call me."

"If it's based on what others call you, I'd say your nickname is Pretentious Git," Precious said. "We can call you Git for short."

I grinned at her.

He shrugged again and turned back to the TV. "At least you'll remember me. It's better to stand out, make your mark."

I frowned at him. Standing out was the last thing I wanted to do. "Do you think we'll get bitten every week?"

"Not me," said Precious. "I'm ready for the next time. And I've got garlic nuts. No way they'll bite me after I've snacked on them."

"You can lick these nuts." Tristan motioned to his crotch before holding his hand up for a high five.

Precious shook her head at him. I ignored him and tuned back into the video where the man had moved on to telling us not to wear silver to the office because it harmed vampires and werewolves.

"How many werewolves do you think there's likely to be in audit?"

Precious shook her head. "No idea. This is the first training I've had."

The man finished with a big thumbs up and informed us we had a test to take. I clicked through the answers on the DVD.

"What shall we watch next?" Tristan asked. "Financial Crime or How to Lift Boxes?"

They both sounded awful.

Chapter 9

Relaxation is important. When you've lived through a few centuries, you realise how easy it is to burn out trying to experience and achieve everything at once.

Elizabeth Bathory – *The First Disrupter*

I slumped onto the saggy sofa back at our new flat and closed my eyes to block out the jumble of boxes that surrounded me.

"So, how was the first day?" Abby unwrapped a stack of pots and shoved them into a cupboard.

I winced as I noticed she'd put them in handle first. "Not what I expected."

"Oh?"

The problem with being friends with an agony aunt is that they are good listeners. You can't fob them off with one liners and expect them to drop a topic. Even if there were a ton of boxes to unpack.

"My laptop didn't work, then I spent the whole day watching videos about how not to commit fraud…which was strange because they gave quite a few examples of how to do it…and a vampire bit me." I pointed to the yellow plaster on my neck. Albert had told us to keep them on for the rest of the week to make sure we weren't targeted by any of his enthusiastic senior managers and had given us a supply of six more.

"They can't do that!"

"They can. I signed a contract."

"They can't put that in a legal document."

"They can. I checked." It was there in black and white, under the benefits section with clear limits on how much blood could be drained – half a pint or two hundred and eighty-four millilitres – and how often. At least I knew no one would try to suck me for another week. "How did it go here?"

"I wrote up a couple of blog posts and an article for that woman's magazine and then I started on the boxes. I'm almost done with the kitchen, then it's onto my bedroom. What do you want to eat tonight?"

I grimaced at her mention of the kitchen, knowing I'd have to reorganise it all to my standards and I could feel the need to sort it out washing over me through the tiredness of the day. Sometimes I wished I was normal and could ignore the gnawing need to have everything the way I liked it. "Takeaway."

"I was hoping you'd say that." Abby grinned. "I got us

menus for the local Chinese."

She thrust a menu in my face and I studied it, making my standard selection of sweet and sour chicken with egg fried rice and a side of spring rolls to share. Abby nodded and disappeared into her bedroom to place the order.

I checked on my pet and gave him his dinner of seeds and carrots. "Nibbles, what have I done?"

The large black and white hamster paused from nibbling his seeds. I reached down and stroked his small head.

"I wanted somewhere to belong, but no one wants me there."

Nibbles turned back to his food, and I withdrew my hand from his cage before he got bitey.

"You're right, it's just going to take some time to adjust. I can't expect to fit in after one day. Good talk."

I left him to his dinner and set up a large cardboard box for us to use as a table – the actual table was loaded with more boxes than I was prepared to deal with right now.

The food arrived so fast it was almost magic until I remembered we lived above the restaurant. Abby handed out the cartons and sat down on the sofa with a sigh. I inhaled the tangy scent of Chinese food, it smelled great, and my mouth watered at the anticipation of a crispy spring roll.

"Any crazies in the inbox today?" I asked, making small talk as I cut the roll in two. "I think they left off one of the rolls. The menu said it was two in a portion." I frowned at the plastic container holding a singular spring roll.

"Crazier than you, you mean?"

"Hey!" I threw a fortune cookie at her. She caught it with a laugh. Wanting to get what you'd ordered was normal, wasn't it. And the menu had definitely said a portion was two spring rolls. Now we had to share, which was fine. Totally fine.

"I only get mail from people who are worried their partner is cheating on them or wondering why they can't find love. I've got a new system: the thought cake." She used her hands to emphasise the phrase. "It's where I tell people they need to look beyond the outside layer of icing to the deeper meaning in the creamy centre. What do you think?"

"It sounds like psychobabble to me. So…" I grinned, "perfect for your readers."

She sank back against a box. "I thought so too." Abby eyed me. "Do you want me to run downstairs and ask for another spring roll?"

"No." I'd cut it now.

"Cool. Do you want to watch *Makeovers on a Budget* or *Celebrity Baker*?"

"*Celebrity Baker* for sure." I ate my food, wiping my hands between bites as the formulaic programme lulled me into a sense of security. How bad could things be in a world where celebrities showed off their lack of baking skills for the world to watch?

After it had finished, Abby cleared up by dumping the takeaway containers in the recycling. I winced. She hadn't rinsed them out.

"OK, I've got to sort out at least part of my bedroom or I'll be sleeping on boxes. You should do the same."

"I will, just going to look over the kitchen first."

She raised an eyebrow at me. "Do you want to thought cake that with me?"

"Nothing to thought cake here. I'm stressed and tired, and I need the comfort of knowing where you've put everything."

"OK, don't stay up too late."

Famous last words. I was up until three a.m sorting out the kitchen, wiping down cupboards, and, yes, I rinsed out the takeaway boxes.

Chapter 10

Every day is full of surprises. Make sure you're the largest surprise there is.

Elizabeth Bathory – *The First Disrupter*

The first week at the Bathory Corporation passed both slowly and quickly. There were endless induction videos and compliance tests to make sure we understood the proper way to log incidents and stack files, interspersed with mindless tasks that the established team members enjoyed tormenting us with. Today, I was on scanning duty.

Debbie had patiently explained how to use the photocopier / scanner / printer that sat enclosed within screens in the middle of the office; put the paper in, make sure the lid was fully closed and press the grey button to scan or the green button to photocopy. Simple. I yawned as I placed the first piece of paper into the scanner plate. It had been a long week at home too, but we were down to five boxes and the kitchen and bathroom were exactly how I liked them. There was a strange water stain on one wall that I'd left Abby to sort, but other than that, the flat was great. For a tiny place on the outskirts of London. My commute was over an hour, and I'd taken to snoozing on the train home, which had taken me two stops in the wrong direction last night and did not help my lack of sleep. But my first paycheck was three weeks away. Not that I was counting.

I pressed the button for five copies. The photocopier / printer beeped, but nothing happened.

"Come on." I pushed the button again.

"Try pressing the red and green button together," came a deep voice from behind me. I turned and smiled at the newcomer. He looked a couple of years older than me, dressed in a navy-blue suit with matching tie and polished shoes. No fangs that I could see.

"Thanks."

"No problem, are you new here?" He leaned on one of the grey screens that shut the printer off from the rest of the room and eyed me.

"Just started on the grad scheme. I'm in Fae Audits."

"Me too. Just back from one, actually."

"Really?" This was my first chance to understand more about what a fae audit meant. I pressed the buttons he indicated and turned back. "What did you get up to?"

He'd gone. Weird behaviour. Behind me, the printer rattled

and clacked. I jabbed at the cancel button as the machine rocked from side to side. A jet of black ink cascaded out of a slot and covered me. I stood there, unsure what had happened or what to do when I heard the sniggering. I turned slowly and there was the newcomer, howling with laughter.

"What the hell?"

"I cannot believe you fell for that. The wall…it's perfect."

I eyed the white silhouette – my silhouette – surrounded by black ink now on the wall. Great.

"OK, team, gather round." Albert's voice sounded through the department. I groaned, but there was no escape. I grabbed a couple of blank pieces of paper and wiped myself down, but the strange ink smudged into my clothes.

"Come on," smirked the newcomer, and he gestured for me to exit the printer's room. I narrowed my eyes and walked past him, doing a fake stumble as I passed and smearing some of the black stains onto him.

"What the hell?" He glared at me. "This is a designer suit."

"Oops," I headed over to where the rest of the audit team had gathered.

"Right, team," Albert rubbed his hands together, "we've got an audit come in. It's a big job, but don't worry, I'll have you all back by the Christmas party." His gaze landed on me and his eyes widened. "What happened to you?"

"Printer," I mumbled.

"Ah. So you've met Percy." His eyes narrowed at the rest of the team. "Didn't anyone tell you about the possessed printer?

No, I suppose not." He let out a world-weary sigh. "Now we'll have to get an engineer out to replace the toner and Debbie will have to play the music."

I glared at Designer Suit who upped his smirk. "It must have slipped my mind."

"OK, well, get yourself cleaned up. We're leaving first thing tomorrow morning. Meet in the lobby at seven a.m. sharp. Debbie! Get the Seventies mix on!" he called.

"Which idiot set him off?" she asked as she got the album up on her phone.

I raised my hand. She rolled her eyes and turned back to her desk as some up-tempo rock ballad blared across the office. I caught sight of myself in the reflection of one of the monitors and winced; I looked like a Rorschach inkblot test. I rubbed at it. That made things worse.

"And, Debbie," Albert added, "see if you can cross-charge the toner to another department."

"On what grounds?" she asked. "I could try for HR because it was a graduate slip up or we could see if Deceased Liaisons could pick up the bill or–"

Albert cut her off just as my eyes started to droop. "Just see to it, please."

That seemed to be the cue for people to leave. I waited for everyone to disperse and took a deep breath, choking on some of the toner ink and ending up in a coughing fit. Albert handed me a bottle of water and waited for me to wash down the sticky, somehow metallic taste of the toner.

"Are you alright, Elle?" He was all fatherly concern.

"I, uh, don't have a passport. I'm sorry, I should have said something earlier–"

He held up a hand. "You don't need a passport to go to the fae realm. Now go home, get cleaned up, and pack."

I grabbed my bag, waved off the sympathetic looks from Precious, ignored the sarcastic jibes from Tristan and headed home to get ready to go to the fae realm.

Chapter 11

A well-placed gesture can often work wonders to calm many waters, but beware of accepting gifts unless you know exactly what they mean.

Elizabeth Bathory – *The First Disrupter*

The next morning, I wheeled my suitcase up the steps to the office, cursing its bulk.

A homeless woman in an oversized coat bent over something on the ground next to the railings. Sympathy swelled my heart. I could afford to be generous; I'd got my dream job and was looking forward to a decent pay cheque in a couple of weeks' time.

I abandoned my suitcase, dug out a tenner from my wallet and walked over.

"Here," I said, holding out the note, ready for the warm rush of gratitude from the beggar and the smug feeling that came from doing a good deed.

"Get lost," said the woman. That was not what I expected. I took a step back. "I don't need charity from them as works for the devil."

Crap. She wasn't homeless. She was a protestor. Now I could see her crude, badly spelled cardboard sign on the floor.

That had been part of our induction. There were always ignorant people who begrudged success, especially from minority groups like supernaturals or from women. And Elizabeth Bathory was both, making her – and her company – a double target. We were instructed to ignore them and never speak to them in case whatever we said ended up quoted in the press.

I backed up to the safety of the steps and retrieved my suitcase.

"Supernaturals go home!" the protestor called.

I made it up the stairs, ignoring her cries, and waited in the large atrium with my wheeled fabric suitcase. The corners were frayed and stood out in the sleek office interior, but it did the job. I was clean and wearing the borrowed purple suit again. My grey one was ruined from the dark toner and I'd had to use the last of my overdraft to buy a replacement that now hung in the suit bag over my shoulder.

Tristan walked out of the office with a smug look on his face. "Enjoy your lie in?"

It was five to seven. "Albert said meet at seven."

"He said be in the lobby at seven. I've been at work for an hour already. Got to impress the boss to keep your job."

I scowled. Why hadn't I thought of that?

"If you're good at your job, you don't need to rely on cheap tricks like that," Precious said as she joined us. She had come through the office door as well. My shoulders slumped, and I made a mental note to show up earlier next time.

More people walked in, crossing paths with the vampires heading home before the sun got too high. Albert sauntered across the tiles with a coffee in hand, chatting to the suited prick who had tricked me yesterday.

"Good, you're here. This is Edwyn, he's one of my senior managers, and, more importantly for you, he's leading the audit team on the ground."

Tristan barged forward, thrusting his hand at Edwyn. He misjudged the distance and knocked the senior manager's coffee to the ground with a sloshing splat that echoed around the atrium. Every employee in the lobby turned and stared at the growing brown puddle on the ground.

"I am so sorry, let me buy you another one."

Albert waved Tristan away. "We don't have time for that. You'll have to have a coffee when you get there. Come on, or we'll miss our slot."

Edwyn glowered at Tristan but kept silent as we followed Albert to an airy office on the ground floor that was filled with potted plants, some with huge, waxy leaves and others that trailed along the wall and across the ceiling. Something brushed against my shoulder and I had the feeling that the plants were sizing me up. Tristan swatted at a vine and

Precious moved to the centre of the room, as far from the strange greenery as she could get. A floral scent tickled my nostrils under the fresh dampness of the hot room.

"You're late."

I whipped my head round to find the speaker. A small woman leaned against a wall, her green suit blending in with the plants as she sipped from a wooden cup filled with tea. As she pushed herself up and into the sunlight, I noted the pointed ears and too bright eyes that marked her as fae.

"Come on, Pytha," Albert wheedled, "it's only a minute."

"You know the alignments are tricky," the fae snapped.

"I brought you this." He nodded to Edwyn and the younger man stepped up and pulled a box of luxury chocolates from his laptop bag.

Pytha looked him up and down. "Very nice," she said, accepting the chocolates without looking at them. He squirmed under her scrutiny, and I decided that I liked this Pytha.

"How's the prototype going?" Albert picked up a wooden cube from a table that grew out of one wall.

"Put it down." Albert dropped the cube and gave her a sheepish smile. "It's called a prototype for a reason. It's not stabilised, so we're doing this the old-fashioned way. Have you got the forms?"

Again, Edwyn stepped forward and handed her a sheaf of paper. "Lovely," she smiled at him without looking at the forms. "They haven't signed." She gestured to us.

"It's covered by their employment contract."

Pytha raised an eyebrow. "Humour me."

Albert motioned us forward and pointed to the forms. "Sign it."

I took the form and read it, not making the same mistake about missing the small print twice. Plus, she was fae. Everyone knew the rumours, and I was on high alert after the background reading I had done on fae folklore and customs last night. "What's this favour?"

Pytha grinned, showing sharp teeth. "As per clause thirty-two a, the favour is limited to a gift of food or drink unless negotiated separately. I prefer the fae blend tea they sell at the tea shop at Spitalfields, or a box of chocolates never hurts – caramel."

"That favour is covered by the chocolates. One favour per trip, not per team member." Albert wagged his finger at her. "You know better than to try to extort our new graduates."

Pytha grinned, unabashed at being caught out. "Unless you'd like to negotiate an alternative…" she suggested to me.

I gulped and shook my head.

"Good, then hurry up. The further we get from dawn, the more power this takes."

I signed and handed the papers to Precious who scrawled her name before passing them to Tristan. She let go before he had them in his hands and the papers tumbled to the floor. He scowled and scrabbled on the floor to retrieve them.

"OK then, let's get this party started." Pytha took a final sip of her tea and abandoned the cup in the crook of a branch. She motioned for us to stand in the doorway and made a complicated series of gestures with her hands. The air thickened and sparked as a shimmering emerald disc appeared under her summoning. It started small – the size of an apple – then grew until it took up half the room. The surface swirled and mesmerised me with glimpses of another place through the moving misty coating that covered its surface.

"Well, go on then. I can't hold this all day," Pytha twisted her hands and there was an audible pop as the glistening disc stabilised into a pulsing oval with tendrils of bright green magic snaking around its edges.

"You're a diamond, Pytha. See you on the return." Albert grabbed his suitcase, stepped into the disc, and disappeared.

Tristan, Precious and I wore mirror expressions of shock, and Edwyn grinned. "Last one through carries my case." He followed the director and vanished.

Precious recovered first. She squared her shoulders and jogged through the portal. I took a step forward, but Tristan pushed me back and went through first. I glared after him, but he'd gone. With a sigh, I stepped through and stopped. A thick cobweb feeling pushed me back, a resistance I wasn't expecting after the others had made it through so easily.

"Interesting," Pytha said, "but I like a challenge." She poured more magic into the portal until it glowed a neon green. She gave me a nod.

The cobweb sensation lightened to a tickle along my skin

and I stepped through. A strange lurching sensation grabbed me and whirled me round before shoving me out the other side. I stumbled onto thick grass and my suitcase collided with the back of my legs, but at least I was standing. Precious sat with her head between her knees and Tristan vomited up his breakfast onto a line of maroon mushrooms.

Albert clapped a meaty hand on my shoulder. "Welcome to the fae realm."

Chapter 12

There is no substitute for hard work. Anyone who tells you different is trying to sell you something.

Elizabeth Bathory – *The First Disrupter*

Above us, the sky flickered in hazy waves of blues, greens and reds over a purplelish blue base. It was beautiful. Under our feet, the ground was spongy and coated with lush green grass. In the distance, I could see glints of moonlight sparkling on an ocean that stretched to the horizon. I turned my face away as my thoughts threatened to dwell on the water and the depths beneath it. How many species of shark lurked under the waves? Great. Now I had a new worry to add to my list. Luckily, we weren't here for swimming. We had a job to do.

Edwyn grinned down at me and shoved a suitcase handle into my hand, breaking my dark thoughts. "Looks like you get the honour of carrying my suitcase. Don't scuff the corners."

I bit my tongue and accepted his case, weighing it along with my own.

A medium height man hurried over to us, his long robe wafting over the tips of the grass.

"Albert, it's been too long." Now he was closer, I could see the pointed ears that marked him as fae, or maybe an elf.

"Only three years, Skathi."

"Ah yes, the triennial audit. How I look forward to those, and this must be your team. How lovely to meet you. May I have your names?"

"Ah, ah." Wagging his finger, Albert stepped in front of our group. "None of that. You know the rules; no bargaining with employees of the Bathory Corporation."

"Naturally. How could I have forgotten?" Skathi held up his hands, but his gaze was sharp as he studied us for a moment before heading down a path.

Albert fell into step with our host and I scurried along behind, dragging my own suitcase and Edwyn's. I made sure his case hit as many rocks along the way as I could without being obvious about it.

"What did he mean?" Tristan asked, panting under all the laptop bags.

"Don't make a bargain with the fae," Precious replied, pulling Albert's case along with her own without any difficulty.

"He only asked what our names were," Tristan said.

"Didn't you hear? He asked if he could have our names." I shuddered. "If we'd given them to him, we'd be under his control. Fae one oh one." It was one of the common tricks I'd read about last night when I researched them. If I was going to the fae realm, I wanted to know what I was getting into. Other tidbits included not accepting food the fae offered and never making any bargains with them.

"Of course, I knew that. I was making sure you did. See you later, losers." Tristan strode on ahead, puffing hard as he yelled for the others to "Wait up!"

They ignored him and continued in conversation with Skathi as they headed for a large manor house surrounded by rolling fields with blue-green grass waving in the gentle breeze.

I met Precious' eyes. She rolled hers, shrugged and continued in the same direction. There were several smaller houses – huts, if I was being accurate – woven from branches and grass into graceful spheres that glinted gold in the strange light of the fae sky.

Angular faces peered through slitted windows, eyes glittering as they stared at us. A few of the small folk on the road stopped and stared as we passed by. Precious' shoulders tensed and I averted my gaze. Attention was always something I hated; growing up, it had rarely been good to come to anyone's notice. I kept to my tried and tested strategy; head down, work hard and fly under the radar.

A large cart rattled past with maple leaves printed on the wooden boxes. I did a double take at the enormous snail pulling the cart. Its body was a greyish yellow, but its shell shimmered with rainbow pearlescence. It turned one of its four eyes on stalks to stare at us as it slid past, leaving a damp trail of slime in its wake.

I checked my watch, relieved to see the second hand still ticking round. I needed some normality after seeing a snail as big as a horse.

The cart overtook the others and pulled to a stop outside a huge manor where skinny fae started unloading the boxes, giving us sideways glances as they worked. A fae with tattoos all over his body nudged a colleague as we got closer. Clearly humans were not ordinary visitors here.

Skathi walked on, oblivious to the stir we outsiders had caused. He paused for the briefest second outside the manor before the doors opened without him touching them and he strode in as if that was normal.

The manor walls were of the same woven branch and grass construction as the huts, but larger and more oval than spherical. Enormous blue-green leaves lay in an intricate pattern over the roof and wooden shutters hung outside huge glassless windows. Outside the entrance and off to one side was a gigantic circular stone, easily seven feet tall, with the centre cut out so it looked like a huge ring doughnut.

I stopped gaping like a tourist and hurried inside to join the others. A silent fae stood on either side of the door and they stepped up behind us, heads bowed in a posture of servitude.

"Amazing. Reminds me of my trip to the Bahamas," Tristan said to no one in particular.

"Indeed," replied the fae, taking a carved statue of a curvaceous woman from Tristan's hands and replacing it on a decorative table. "I have allocated rooms for your work, with guest bedrooms for sleeping attached in the east wing. Allow me to show them to you."

Albert inclined his head and Skathi led us to the rooms. The grass doors were woven in an intricate spiral design that mimicked the Fibonacci sequence to perfection. Inside the main room were three long tables that looked like they had been grown from the ground, with small twigs bearing leaves curling off the legs and corners.

Albert nodded to Tristan, who unloaded the laptop bags onto the table.

"Your rooms are through there," Skathi said, pointing to a narrow corridor off this room. "I'll let you get settled in."

"We'd prefer to start straight away," Albert said, rubbing his hands together.

"But you must have tea first, I insist."

"Skathi…" There was a note of warning in Albert's voice.

The fae sighed. "Always so suspicious. Here." With a flourish, he produced a scroll from somewhere in his robes and handed it to Albert. "A guarantee that I expect nothing in return for my hospitality and that the food is safe."

"And the drink?"

Skathi's smile didn't meet his large eyes. "Naturally." He took a quill from another secret pocket and made a note on the scroll. "There. Anything you eat or drink in my house will not cause you harm or tie you to me in any way. Is there anything else?"

Albert shook his head and passed the scroll to me.

"Then I will leave you with Frigja and Havul. They can get you anything you need."

"Just the records for the past three years, please."

"Naturally, and I'll send in the tea."

Once Skathi had left, with the two serving fae in tow, Albert breathed a sigh of relief. "OK team, here's the plan. This is the triennial audit and fae records are thorough, so we are going to work through any scrolls they bring us and compare them to the annual record of the island's cashflow. That will take the majority of the time, then you'll perform a physical asset test against the record of assets and we'll sign off the accounts for the Emperor before Winter Solstice."

"Skathi's a king?" Tristan asked, a note of disbelief lacing his voice.

"No. Skathi governs this island on behalf of the Unseelie Court." One of many fae courts I'd discovered in my reading. "Emperor Llyr rules the courts and will accept our audit before we leave. So, let's make this thorough. Trust me, you do not want to get on Emperor Llyr's bad side." He shuddered. "Right, get your suitcases in your rooms and let's crack on."

I took my case, leaving Edwyn's by the door, and strode through the second set of woven doors to the bedrooms. Three doors led off a small corridor that sported a large painting of

Skathi wearing something a lot more revealing than the robes he'd greeted us in.

I pushed open the first set, revealing a large room with moss-coated walls and a woven reed carpet. Two single beds made of twisting vines hung from the ceiling.

I looked at Precious and raised my eyebrows. "Guess we're sharing."

She eyed the beds with a look of distrust.

"Cool, we're roomies," Tristan said as he held up a hand to high five Edwyn. I caught Edwyn's eye and couldn't help my smile. It looked like he was in his own personal brand of hell. Karma did exist. And it took the form of having to sleep with that idiot.

I grinned as I shut the door. Edwyn and Tristan deserved each other. I checked out the rest of the room. Two decent sized wardrobes grew from the floor – actual trees growing into furniture! – and there was another door off to the right; a bathroom. There was a decent sized shower, toilet and sink, all made of some sort of dark wood and the walls were panelled with a lighter wood that smelled of saunas and sap. It was the nicest room I had ever stayed in.

After freshening up and hanging up our clothes, I unrolled the scroll Albert had shoved at me. Flowing script filled it and I squinted at the unfamiliar calligraphy.

"This is actually a guarantee that we're safe in Skathi's home and the food and drink are safe."

Precious shrugged. "They're fae." As if that explained

anything. "I thought all the warnings were over the top when Mum told me fairy stories, but…looks like it's all true."

I rolled up the scroll, and we headed back into the main room to find tea laid out for us and a heap of scrolls set on the table. Tristan strode in and poured himself a cup from the ceramic teapot decorated with painted maple leaves.

"I've never had tea with maple syrup before." He picked up a small glass jug of syrup that sat next to the teapot on the tray and shook it.

Albert came in and dashed to the table, wrestling the jug from Tristan's hand. "Have you had any?" There was a note of panic in his voice, and Tristan shook his head. Albert sighed, and the tension ebbed from his body. He put the jug back on the tea tray. "Do not drink the maple syrup."

"Why not?"

"It's a form of fae currency," I said, the knowledge fresh in my mind after my research last night.

Albert shot me a tight smile. "And it could be construed as a bribe," he explained. "It's the equivalent of a gold bar in fae terms. We have to be above board here." He took off his suit jacket and hung it on the back of the chair. "OK people, now the work begins."

Chapter 13

Dear Abby, I think my work is taking advantage of me. I work weekends with little notice and no extra pay and there's no sign of promotion. I'm constantly asked to do more, and I feel I can't say no. Don't get me wrong, I'm not a slacker, but other places don't seem to demand this level of commitment. What should I do?

Honey, you sent me a much longer letter so let's thought cake some of these feelings. You say you can't say no (that's the icing thought), but what would be the impact if you did (layer one)? Maybe you'd get some respect from your colleagues and your bosses and some of your free time back. It sounds like you're tying your self-worth to this job (gooey centre) and, honey, that's not OK. Take back some control, say no, and if you do lose your job, well there are more out there and I know you can find one that will give you the respect you deserve.

Yours cakefully, Abby.

Abby Wright – *Ask Abby*

My shoulders dropped as I stepped over the threshold into our small flat and inhaled the stale smell of lemon scented cleaning products. It had been a long week filled with paperwork, and my brain hurt from all the tricky wording the fae used to avoid loopholes in their contracts. All I wanted to do was lie in my own bed and watch some bad TV. But first I checked in on Nibbles.

The greedy hamster scurried out of his house at the sound of food hitting his bowl and took a half-hearted bite at my fingers.

"I missed you, too. Sorry I've been gone so long. It's just work, and I know Abby takes good care of you."

He gave me a sulky look, turned his back on me and did a few laps in the red wheel on the side of his cage. He stopped after six rotations. My jaw tightened. Sometimes I thought he tried to wind me up – six was my unlucky number – but I was tired and giving too much credit to a rodent.

The sound of running water stopped and two minutes later, Abby stepped out of our shared bathroom wearing a huge fluffy towel.

"Elle! You're alive!" She ran over and enveloped me in a soapy, wet hug.

"I've only been gone a week."

"Yes, but you ignored my proof of life messages."

"They seemed passive aggressive."

"You got my articles then."

"On worker rights or the fake agony aunt letter?"

"Oh, it was real. I wondered if one of your co-workers wrote it. What did you think of my response?"

"You're really doubling down on this thought cake thing."

"Yep. My editor loved it and wants Ask Abby as a regular feature – now I've got two columns a week as a freelancer and my vlog gained a hundred followers last week, so I'm monetised! I'm thinking I could do a recipe book interspersing heartfelt letters with tasty recipes."

"You don't bake."

"An insignificant detail. Besides, that's what the internet's for."

I rubbed my eyes. Her enthusiasm was hard to take when I had such low energy. I wasn't sure how I'd make it to my phone to order a pizza.

"Anyway, dinner's on me. I bet you're exhausted."

I nodded.

"Good, there's a new Thai place opened on the corner I want to try. I'll order something."

"I don't know any Thai dishes." My heart rate spiked as she dropped her phone with the menu page open into my lap. I had a technique for ordering out; pick familiar dishes after much research into the menu, but now she had sprung a new cuisine on me. I scrolled down until I spotted the dishes with noodles and forced myself to relax as I read the descriptions, settling on a pad thai.

"Great choice. Shall we share?"

I groaned. "What if I don't like yours?"

"Just try it. You might be surprised."

I folded my arms and turned on the TV. *Not likely.*

"So, how's work?" Abby asked after she'd placed the order.

I shrugged, still grappling with the new food options. Why couldn't we stick to what we knew? And the Chinese place downstairs was good even if they did scrimp on the spring rolls. "Not much to tell, lots of paperwork. It's my first audit, so I don't know if that's normal or not. We have to check over a hundred scrolls to do with asset transfers and these collateralised deals that were there in the last audit. And their handwriting is worse than yours."

"Who writes nowadays? Everything's typed. Why do you have to check all those scrolls if they got checked last time?"

"Because that's what they did in the last audit."

"You know that makes no sense, right?"

We stared at each other for a while, neither comprehending each other until Abby shrugged. "And how's the fae realm?"

"Colourful."

"Colourful? That's all I get? You have the chance to visit a magical realm that most people can only dream of and it's 'colourful'." She dropped the air quotes around the word with precision.

"Didn't you get the picture I sent you?"

"Yeah, but what's it like?"

"The sky is purple with these weird lights flickering across it, like the aurora borealis on that nature documentary we watched when we lost the remote. Everything's made of plants, but I'm not there as a tourist, I'm stuck in a room for most of the day looking at paperwork, or maybe you could call it scroll work because most of it's written on these rolled up leaves."

"Cool. Can humans visit?"

"I don't think they've got a tourist board, but I'll ask. Happy?"

I rubbed my eyes again with one hand, while the other one twitched. Abby caught the motion.

"You can start stress cleaning after dinner. I left you the bathroom."

"Thank you so much."

"Don't get sarcastic with me. You only get annoyed if I do it."

"You don't scrub the grout," I grumbled. She gave me an I-told-you-so look and I couldn't help but grin. "Thanks for looking after Nibbles while I was away."

"No problem. I only almost lost a finger."

"I told you not to put your hand in the cage."

"He's a demon rat."

"So, you won't look after him for me?" My heart sunk into my sensible work shoes. Without anyone to look after my pet, I couldn't stay away for more than a night at a time. Maybe there was some sort of timer I could sort for his food, but what about fresh water? And I liked to clean out his cage twice a week so he had fresh bedding and toilet sand..

Her eyes softened, and she placed her hand over mine. "Of course I'll look after him for you. But if he bites, I'm putting him on the cheapest food I can find."

"Do you hear that, Nibbles? Stay on Abby's nice side if you want to keep your premium food privileges." He gave a squeaky grunt. "He says he'll be good."

"I'll believe it when I see it." An electronic buzzing filled the flat. I jumped before I remembered we had a buzzer now. "Food!" Abby got up to collect it and we sat and ate out of the cartons while watching the latest *Celebrity Baker* as Abby's head filled with dreams of her recipe book and she commented on every single dish. Every. Single. One.

Chapter 14

Why try to fit into a world that isn't made for you? I prefer to stand out and mould the world to fit me.

Elizabeth Bathory – *The First Disrupter*

Monday rolled around too quickly, and I was back at the office at half six, ready for our seven a.m portal transfer. I decided to set up in the Fae Audits department for a bit, mainly to rub Tristan's upturned nose in me getting here before he did. When I got to my desk, I noticed a laptop open on his desk, the screensaver blinking as the Bathory Corporation's bat crest logo bounced around the screen.

My fist clenched around my bag. He'd beaten me in, the creeping little… The object of my ire walked in with a yawn.

"Glad you could make it, Speckle."

"How?"

"Hmmm? I guess some of us are just more dedicated than

you are."

"But…"

"Ah, ah," he shook a sarcastic finger at me, "you've only got yourself to blame for your tardiness."

I slammed my laptop bag down on the desk, connected up the computer and scanned through my emails. Fred the vampire – the same one who'd bitten me on my first day and who I had avoided since – walked past us, heading home after a long night at the office.

"OMG! How did I not notice before? You look exactly like that bloke from the Office," Tristan shrieked.

"I beg your pardon?"

"The Office. The TV programme. Speckle, don't you think he looks like the manager from the show?"

I turned away, not wanting to get involved with Tristan's inanities.

"Never heard of it," the vampire said, heading for the door.

"You've never heard of it? Come on! It's a classic, real vintage vibes. You have to watch it. I'm getting it up right now." He tapped on his keyboard and showed one of the more famous scenes to the bemused vampire. "Seriously, you have to watch it."

"Hmmm." With that, the vampire left.

I shook my head. "You know they monitor our search histories, right?"

Tristan swore and closed down the YouTube clip. "What's

that for?"

"What?"

"The head shake."

With a sigh, I turned to him. "Do you really think that annoying people is going to help you fit in?"

"I don't want to fit in." He looked at me like I'd grown an extra head. "I want to get on, climb the ladder, get a directorship."

"You're going to annoy people into promoting you?" I guess that was a tactic…if it got him out of the department, I could get on board with it, even though it went against every one of my instincts that screamed hard work should get rewarded rather than whatever Tristan was doing.

"I'm memorable. What have you got?" He gestured to me. "Grey suit, soft voice, weird speck near your ear. You blend in. No one will remember you. But me? I'm making sure everyone knows my name and sharing some great programming advice with a senior worker. He'll thank me."

I snorted and got back to the emails. If that was his plan, he'd be gone by Christmas. No one liked a noisy show off. But, as Albert came in and Tristan stood to shake his hand, I wondered if I was right or if Tristan and his stupid in-your-face approach actually worked.

Edwyn entered behind Albert, carrying a tray of drinks.

"Coffees on me," Albert said with a smile.

"Great!" Tristan grabbed the nearest one, took a sip and grinned. "Caramel shot. Nice." He held up his hand for a high five.

Edwyn glowered at him. "That was my drink."

"Sorry, do you want it?"

I bit my lip to stop myself laughing at Edwyn's face. "No. I do not want a drink that you've slobbered into. Didn't you see my name on the side?"

Tristan studied his paper cup. "Oh, yep. There it is. Hey, we're coffee buddies."

"We are not buddies," Edwyn replied through gritted teeth.

"I'll run down and get you another one."

Albert shook his head. "There isn't time. You'll have to have one of the plain ones, Edwyn."

Precious barged into the room, slightly out of breath.

"Now we're all here, let's go," Albert continued. "Do you have the chocolates for Pytha?"

Edwyn nodded and shoved his suitcase at Tristan before sweeping out of the door after Albert.

"Tell me what I missed," Precious asked as I stuffed my laptop back into its bag.

"Just Tristan pissing Edwyn off."

She grinned and clapped me on the back. "Excellent, better ratings for us. Weekend?"

"I spent my one free day making sure my clothes were clean, and I binge watched *Celebrity Baker* season one. You?"

"Saw the family, washed clothes, slept and ended up dreaming about those stupid contracts."

"How many more do you think we'll need to go through?"

"Don't ask."

This time, Pytha took the chocolates with a murmured "Delicious." I wasn't sure if she was salivating over the confectionary or Edwyn in his black suit with a tie that matched his eyes. How long did the man spend picking out his clothes to get that level of coordination?

Portal travel was easier on my stomach this time and the lurching sensation wasn't quite as bad as the first time I'd gone through. When I opened my eyes, we were back in the fae realm. I took a moment to check my watch and get some reassurance that this was all real and not some dream where the aurora borealis shone in the daytime before Albert marched us straight to the mansion, ready to work.

Chapter 15

People love power. Give them a little, but not too much and they'll be so intoxicated, they'll do anything for you.

Elizabeth Bathory – *The First Disrupter*

"OK team, I'm leaving Edwyn in charge while I head back to head office for Board meetings. I'll see you on Monday morning, bright and early and if you need anything, you can always contact me via email."

A nasty smile played on Edwyn's lips as Albert stepped out of the room. I should have known something was up when our director hadn't brought a suitcase.

"You all heard Albert. Now, I think it's time to start on the physical assets check while I carry on with these scrolls."

"Tell us what you want us to do." Precious folded her arms and met Edwyn's gaze with a confidence that I could never match.

"Simple. Here's a map of the island. You'll see all the fae stones used to guarantee contracts marked. I want you to check they all exist."

I studied the scale and frowned. "This will take weeks."

"Not my problem."

"Is checking them all really the best use of our time? How about a sample test?" I tried again.

"Aww, someone's been reading up on their audit terms." Edwyn shot me a condescending look. "But, I'm in charge of this audit, not you, and if I ask you to do a thorough physical asset examination, you do it. In fact, if I ask you to jump, you say—"

"How high?" Tristan interrupted and won a smile from Edwyn.

"He gets it. So, Tristan can be in charge. Off you go." He took a sip of his tea, grimaced and put it down. As we left, he mumbled, "What I wouldn't give for a bloody coffee."

Tristan took charge of the map and marched us out of the manor house and up to the huge grey doughnut stone right outside. "Right. Here's the first one, tick that off."

"Shouldn't we measure it?" I regretted asking the question as soon as the words were out of my mouth.

"Why?"

"The fae use different sizes and materials for the value of the stone. Part of an asset test is to check that things are where they're meant to be."

"It's a rock." Tristan gave me a you-cannot-be-serious look.

Precious backed me up. "She's right. The combination of size and the deeper or more unusual colour, the more it's worth. We should make sure the right collateral has been used."

The fae currency system was complex, but essentially, the fae on this island transferred stones to each other in exchange for goods and service, much like any other currency, except, the rocks didn't change location. Instead, the ownership changed and was recorded in the island's primary ledger. Something we'd have to check once we'd made sure the stones all existed and were where they were meant to be.

The upshot was that someone could own any of the fae stones anywhere on the island as long as both the seller and the purchaser and the governor agreed that the stone existed. In theory, having three people involved in every transaction meant it was less liable to fraud, but it was part of our job to check.

"Did you bring a tape measure?" Tristan sneered, unwilling to lose face and admit he knew next to nothing about the fae monetary system.

I tapped on my phone and brought up a measuring app before pointing it at the rock. I jotted the measurements down and asked him for the coordinates. He squinted at the map before Precious plucked it from his hands, turned it round, and handed it back to him. Tristan scowled and read out the coordinates. I recorded them in my lined notebook. One down. Fifty more to go.

After the third stone – a gorgeous russet one that shimmered under the pearlescent colours of the fae sky, just outside the town that the manor was on the outskirts of – Tristan squinted at the map. "This is going to take forever."

"Yep." I wrote down the diameter of this one.

"OK," he mused, "so we split up."

"I don't think that's a good idea…"

"I'm in charge, right? And I think it's a great idea. We'll cover more ground. Take a picture of this map and we'll all download that measuring app. You go to the West. I'll go east. Precious, go south and meet back at the manor at sundown."

"We still won't get everything done."

"Nope, but it's good initiative and we'll get through it quicker. And more importantly, I asked you to do something, so do it."

"You don't get to tell us what to do," Precious jabbed a finger at Tristan's suit.

"Edwyn put me in charge, which means, yeah, I get to tell you what to do. So, do it, or I'll write you a bad peer assessment for the Reaping."

Precious raised one eyebrow and flicked her braids over her shoulder.

I stepped forward before this turned into a fight. "It's OK. The quicker we can do it, the quicker we can get back to the manor. Come on, we'll walk out together."

"Fine." She stalked off down the south west path and I

followed her, trotting to keep up with her longer legs. "I hate that prissy prick. Telling us what to do. I'll show him what to do."

"It's fine. Look," I pointed at a cart pulled by a strange striped creature that was a cross between a sabre-tooth tiger and a horse. "Maybe we can get a lift."

Her face brightened and she strode over, turning on a smile that got the owner to agree to let us on their cart. The driver said they'd take us to the next stone so I climbed on, enjoying the warm breeze on my face as he took us down the track to a dark blue circular stone that was twice as tall as Precious. I wrote down the coordinates while Precious measured.

"Time to split," she said.

I eyed the tiger horse that pawed the ground in a nearby field. "Will you be alright?"

Precious grinned at me and hiked up her skirt to reveal a dagger strapped to her thigh. "I never go anywhere without my clan dirk."

"Dirk?" I asked weakly.

"Dagger."

"Of course."

"Don't worry so much. See you back at the manor."

"See you later." Even as I spoke, Precious started striding off.

Time to make a plan. There was no way I'd get the entire western side of the island done today, and if I'd had time, I could have worked out the most efficient way for us to tackle this, but I didn't want to rock the boat, so I headed out in a straight line to the coast, noting down each fae stone I passed on the way.

Soon I was on a white beach, my shoes slipping on the perfect sand. I inhaled, breathing in the salty tang of the sea air. It was the sort of cove Abby dreamed of for a holiday destination, but I was at work, so I tore my gaze away from the azure sea and scanned the beach for the fae stone.

A frown creased my forehead, and I tapped my pen on the notebook before turning back to my photo of the map. Zooming in, I saw that there should have been a stone somewhere here; a big one, worth a fortune in fae currency. After half an hour scrabbling over sand and peering behind every dune, I had to accept defeat. I marked the location in my notebook and scrawled a large question mark next to it.

Pursing my lips, I studied the map again. The next stone was too far away for me to make it before the sky faded into the darker blue-black of night. With a sigh, I trudged back to the manor.

I was the first one of our trio to make it back, and Edwyn looked up from a long scroll and raised an eyebrow before turning back to the contract. "How did it go?" he asked.

"Good. We made a good start. Ummm."

He looked up again. "I want to finish this scroll today, so whatever you're not saying. Say it."

"I couldn't find one of the fae stones."

"Then you weren't looking hard enough."

I moved closer and showed him the map on my phone. "This one down at the beach wasn't there. I looked everywhere."

He frowned and took my phone from me before rooting around in the pile for a map of the island. The one he found was subtly different from the one Tristan had. Edwyn studied it, the line between his eyebrows deepening until he let out a bark of laughter.

"It's there alright."

I tilted my head to better see the cause of his merriment. I gulped. "It's underwater?"

"The tides or a storm must have changed the coastline." He tapped the map thoughtfully and the smile he turned on me was cruel. "But the fae don't care about the location. As long as the stone exists, they can still use it as collateral and exchange it like any other stone. So, you're going to make sure it's there."

I squeaked, but that made his smile widen. "I don't have a swimming costume."

"It's not my fault you're not prepared. Go back out there and look for it."

"I'll go in the morning."

"Now." The threat of a bad assessment where I was cited for insubordination and not following simple instructions loomed between us.

I glared at him before schooling my face into a more pleasant expression. It was unfair, but he could help or hinder at the Selection Ceremony, and I didn't want to lose this job. I swallowed and made my way to the bedroom I shared with Precious.

"Where are you going?" he asked.

"To get a change of clothes before I go swimming."

"Smart choice."

He had to get the last word in. I thought uncharitable thoughts as I grabbed some spare underwear and headed back out to the beach.

Chapter 16

I always make time to fit exercise into my daily routine. A healthy body leads to a healthy mind.

Elizabeth Bathory – *The First Disrupter*

I stood at the edge of the water, the warm waves lapping at my bare toes. *Here goes nothing.* I waded in, thankful that the sea was warm – the same temperature as if you'd run a bath and left it for twenty minutes – and that I was alone. I had stripped down to my sensible black underwear and placed my set of clothes set up near one of the grassy dunes, ready for when this nightmare was over. I stroked a finger over my Lilo and Stitch watch. At least that was waterproof up to a depth of thirty metres or so the packaging had claimed when I'd opened it. I took a deep breath and waded out into the sparkling sapphire sea.

Once the water was up to my chest, I paused. This was it. The moment I had to start swimming. Fear gripped my heart in an icy vice as a large wave pulled my feet from the sea floor. I wasn't great at swimming. The state-sponsored swimming lessons at school ensured I could do enough to stay afloat, but no one thought to spend money on private lessons for foster kids. Especially not the homes I'd stayed at. But that was the past.

I was here, now, in a well-paid job, making something of myself and if I had to do a bit of swimming to prove myself, I would. I kicked off the sea bed and did a few strokes out into the ocean. The sky had dimmed from violet to a bruised purple. Night was falling, and I did not want to be stuck out here in the dark. I shivered. What if there were things under the water? I gulped and swallowed a mouthful of briny water. I had to put those thoughts out of my mind and get this job done, before anything came to investigate the stranger swimming in the water.

Turning back to land, I tried to gauge where the sunken rock would be. It wasn't too far, I must be almost above it. I took a deep breath and forced myself to dive. The salt water stung my eyeballs, but I kept them open, scanning the ocean floor for the fae rock. The ocean was clear, free from pollution or mud, and a school of sunshine yellow fish swam past, followed by a dog-sized seahorse that looked like it was made of rose quartz. Beautiful but not a fae stone. I broke the surface, gulping down the cool air. Someone waved at me from the shore. It was too far to make out who the silhouetted figure was, and I gave a small wave back before striking out further into the ocean.

I dived again and resurfaced with no sign of the damned rock. If this was a joke, it wasn't funny. I turned for land. I didn't want to admit defeat, but there was a limit to what was a reasonable ask and I reckoned I'd passed it as soon as I'd stepped into the water. I kicked out and something grazed my leg.

Kicking wildly, I aimed for the shore. *It's just seaweed.* I hoped that was true, but the slimy thing wrapped around my ankle and yanked me under. I screamed, and the sea swallowed me.

Twisting, I kicked out at whatever had me and saw an inky black tentacle wrapped around my lower leg. That was weird, it didn't feel slimy anymore, it was more like pins and needles. In a shot of clarity, I realised that was part of its killing technique. It had numbed by leg so I couldn't fight.

I kicked again with my free leg, colliding with rubbery skin. But the tentacle didn't budge. It was relentless and, amid its pulsating black tentacles writhing beneath me, I spied a razor-sharp beak shaped mouth. My heart hammered in my chest, and I screamed again, letting out the last of my precious air. I pulled with my arms in some sort of crawl stroke, desperate to get to the surface, but it was too strong. Through the clear water, the aurora borealis shimmered in the darkening sky. I thrashed again, but I could feel the poison spreading through my left leg. And, as it pulled me further into the depths, I took a breath and water filled my lungs.

~

"You are not going to die on me. You're the only decent person in the whole damn company. Do not die."

Those were the words I woke up to as I rolled onto my side and coughed up lungful after lungful of salty water in burning vomits.

"You're alive." Precious sat back on her heels then clapped my back so hard my bones rattled.

I spluttered out some more water and pushed myself to my knees, trembling from the cold or the near-drowning, I didn't know. I nodded at her, mouthing a thank you. She'd saved my life.

"Let's get back. I'm done with work for today."

I nodded and wobbled to my feet, my left leg collapsing under me.

"I got you." Precious slipped her arm around my back, lending me her strength.

"My clothes…"

Precious scanned the shoreline. Her jaw clenched. There was no sign of my clothes. Maybe they'd blown away. And now I could think, I realised she was in her underwear, too. We'd both left our suits on the shore and now they were gone. Even my spare set had disappeared.

She tugged me forwards. "Let's get back. We've got more clothes at the manor."

A fae with a cart sat parked just beyond the dunes. Two huge cat-horse beasts pawed the ground, hitched to the cart. Precious bundled me aboard and nodded to the driver. We set off in silence.

I'd almost died. The words whispered through my mind. I hugged my shivering body tighter. Precious kept her arm around my naked shoulders the entire way back.

The manor came into view surrounded by flags on tall sticks flapping in the gentle breeze. It took me a minute to process it. There weren't flags there before. As we got closer, the shape became clearer; our clothes.

Precious jumped off the cart and marched into the manor, unashamed of her white underwear. I followed her, my hands covering as much of my body as they could.

Precious barged through the double doors into our workroom. "Tell me what the hell you think you're playing at."

Edwyn spat his mouthful of tea out over some scrolls, swore and bent over to mop it up. Tristan snickered in a corner. Precious marched into his personal space wearing only her matching bra and pants, which were dangerously close to being see through thanks to rescuing me from the sea.

"Precious!" Edwyn had got his breath back. "What is the meaning of this?"

"Ask him." She jutted out her jaw, baring her tusks and pointed at Tristan.

"Well?"

"What?" Tristan shrugged. "I saw some clothes on the beach and brought them back here to dry."

"I'm not here to deal with disputes between graduates. And

you," Edwyn jabbed a finger at Tristan, "are not in High School. We don't prank colleagues by stealing clothes. You can get them back and pay for dry cleaning."

"I don't care about the bloody clothes." Precious' jaw twitched. "You left Elle out there to die."

Edwyn blanched. "She's dead."

I stepped through the doorway, staring at my feet so I didn't have to meet their gazes, my arms wrapped around my skinny body hiding what I could of my soaking underwear.

Edwyn let out a breath of relief, probably because he'd have to deal with a negative assessment if I'd died out there.

Precious moved in front of me, shielding me from their gaze. "She could have been killed. There're monsters in the water."

"I sent her to find a fae stone, she should have taken precautions," Edwyn said.

Liar. He'd forced me to go. I should have known this place would be just like school. I didn't fit in anywhere.

"She doesn't have any magic. We didn't know about the risks. You could have got her killed." Precious fought on my behalf.

"It's OK, Precious. I just want to get dry."

"See, she's fine." Edwyn turned back to his scrolls.

I scurried to hide in our room.

Precious growled before stalking after me.

"Looking good, Precious," Tristan called. Obnoxious git.

Precious speared him with a look. "Take a good look, pretty boy, because this is the last time you'll get to see my underwear." With that, she tossed her hair and slammed our grass door shut with an anti-climatic hiss.

Chapter 17

People often complain that life isn't fair. And?

Elizabeth Bathory – *The First Disrupter*

I turned off the water and stepped out of the shower. The pins and needles in my leg had dulled to a light tingle and I could walk on it without limping. I wrapped myself in a guest towel that was as soft as a cloud and headed into our shared room before curling up on my bed.

"Atta girl." Precious' voice was gentle and the sudden depression in my bed told me she had sat next to me.

"I feel awful."

"You almost died," she pointed out. "It would be weird not to feel awful."

"Yeah, but I also didn't find the stone."

She laughed. "That's what you're worried about."

"It means we'll have to go back out there."

"Like heck we will."

A timid knock rapped at the door.

"Get lost," Precious replied.

"Come on, we need to debrief." Edwyn's voice came through the door, followed by another knock.

Precious thumped her fist back on the door, making the walls shake. "Not tonight."

I hugged my knees to my chest and closed my eyes. This had all gone so wrong. But I was used to fronting things out.

"Tell them I'll be out in thirty minutes."

"Are you sure?" Precious' gaze was soft, caring. It melted my heart, because all I wanted to do was bury myself in my bedsheets and cry myself to sleep.

Instead, I nodded. She opened the door, relayed the message, and shut it in Edwyn's face with a wicked grin.

"That was satisfying. I'll grab a shower." She sashayed into the bathroom and shut the door with a flick of her foot.

I studied my wardrobe choices. My suit hung outside covered with sand and flapping in the breeze thanks to Tristan's prank, but I had a black dress. That would do. I donned it and stood in front of the mirror. What would Elizabeth Bathory do? She'd go out there without a care in the world and show them she didn't care, that she was strong. Well, so was I. I might not be an orc warrior. But I wasn't some meek child. I was on the graduate scheme at the Bathory Corporation, and I was as tough as any of them.

Thirty-five minutes later, I stared in the mirror again as Precious finished up her braids. She had talked me into borrowing one of her many lipsticks and now my red mouth was all I could look at.

"Are you sure about the colour?"

"Of course, it goes great with your skin. Are you sure you don't want help with your hair?"

I shook my head and pulled it into a high bun – it added a couple of much-needed inches to my height – and reapplied concealer to my birthmark. This was a bad idea. I could feel the compulsion wash over me. I had to do something. I settled for reapplying my lipstick. Seven times.

Precious frowned at me as I layered the colour on but stayed silent. It felt like I was applying war paint, readying me for battle and the anxiety in my chest eased a little. Enough for me to give Precious a nod and we headed out.

In the main room, Tristan and Edwyn sprawled out on chairs. The scrolls had been stacked neatly and next to them was a pile of folded clothes. Our clothes. I clamped my lips shut and stared at them both, daring them to meet my eyes.

"Thank you for coming." Edwyn stood and offered us a drink. "Skathi didn't have a fully stocked bar, but he came through with a few spirits."

Precious pushed his hand away and sniffed each of the bottles before choosing one that looked like scotch. I trusted her and accepted the ceramic cup she gave me, half full of the alcoholic drink. "It's good for shock."

"I wanted to thank you for today. Tristan told me you've made great progress with the stones, so we'll be ahead, which is good. But make sure you're not too far ahead. We're paid by the hour and we've budgeted for two months for this audit, so we need to stick to that deadline."

I frowned. "You want us to work slower?"

"I want us to take the agreed time to finish the audit."

"We're brushing over the fact that Elle almost died today." Precious' nostrils flared as she downed her drink.

"No." Edwyn offered me a printed form. "We take health and safety very seriously. I've pulled an incident form for you to fill in."

Precious snatched the piece of paper from his hand, looked it over, and gave it to me. I scanned it and nodded.

"That's it." Precious opened her mouth to say more, but I stood.

"Leave it, Precious." I couldn't deal with that right now. My lungs still burned. I needed to drink and then pass out on my bed.

"Actually, I'd like to talk to Elle alone for a minute." Edwyn motioned with his head towards the door.

"Looks like it's just you and me and the booze, then Presh." Tristan raised his glass.

"Don't call me that."

I left them bickering and followed Edwyn outside, hugging myself against the chill night air, my drink still in my hand.

Edwyn gazed straight ahead into the darkness of the fae night, lit by a smattering of glowing orbs placed around the manor's grounds. In one of the novels that Abby loved, it would have been the perfect romantic setting. But, I was cold and somewhere between miserable and angry.

"Look, I'm sorry."

I stared at Edwyn. "An apology?"

"That you nearly got killed. Not that I asked you to do your job."

I humphed and took a swig of the honeyed spirit before choking. It was strong and burned my throat on the way down.

Edwyn shot me a smile filled with regret. "The thing about working here is, if you show any weakness, they'll eat you alive." Slimy, conniving git. I almost felt sorry for him.

"Inspiring advice."

"It's not advice. It's a fact and one you should learn sooner rather than later."

"Is that a threat?"

"Just a fact."

I checked my watch. "Are we done here?"

He grabbed my wrist. "What's the deal with the watch?" I gave him a questioning look. "You check it a lot. Did you steal it?"

I yanked my hand away from him. "No!"

"Shame, I thought you might be interesting." Looks like the apology part of the night was over. "So, what's the deal?"

I tapped the glass front seven times without thinking. *How much to tell him?* My mind away from revealing anything about my compulsions. OCD was never something I could adequately explain, and it always ended with mocking or people saying they were a bit OCD too, as if liking things neat and tidy was the same as the irrational thoughts that wormed their way into my brain and could only be kept at bay by rituals. I decided on the sad truth without the craziness added in.

"My first family gave it to me. They were the nicest ones I had, but they got killed in a car accident when I was six, just before they adopted me. It was going to happen on my seventh birthday." I found our Mum – Melanie – had already bought me the watch as a birthday present. It had Lilo and Stitch on the face and it was my favourite film because Ohana means family. And I nearly had one.

"First family?"

"I was fostered. Never made it to adoption after that. Six families in all." I never made it to lucky number seven.

"Sorry to hear it."

"Why? It's not your fault."

A flash of something that might have been humanity passed over his face but then it was gone. "We should get back inside."

I stared after him for a long second before adjusting my watch strap and heading in.

"OK team, let's talk over the plan for tomorrow. You can

get back out and carry on with the physical asset test, and we need to sort out what's going on with the underwater stone."

"There is no underwater stone," I said, surprising myself at the calmness of my voice.

"Maybe you were in the wrong place."

"No way."

He pursed his lips. "You can go back out there."

I folded my arms. "No."

"Are you refusing an order from your supervisor?"

"I'm refusing an unreasonable request. The stone isn't there. Precious and I both checked it, and, as the incident report will say, I nearly drowned and there are monsters in the water, so no, I will not go back." My chest heaved and adrenaline spiked through my body. My hands shook and my stomach roiled. I could not believe I'd just defied a direct order and stood up to a senior colleague. I opened my mouth to take it all back, but Precious stood beside me, backing me up.

"Agreed," she said.

"Fine. Elle, you're on reconciliations with me. Tristan and Precious – physical assets. I'm off to bed." He stormed out of the room and Precious held out her fist. I bumped it, and smiled before a wave of nausea hit me and I dashed to our bathroom.

Abby would have a field day if I wrote into her column about this; *Dear Abby, Today I stood up to my horrible boss and now I'm throwing up. Why am I such a mess?*

Chapter 18

If you have any concerns, escalate to your manager in the first instance.

Bathory Corporation Employee Handbook

After that outburst, I was stuck reconciling contracts for the rest of the week, which Edwyn and I completed in silence until Albert came back for us on Friday. He entered the room balancing a stack of pizza boxes in his arms, and placed them on the table.

"A reward for my audit team. Thanks for doing such a great job this week. Skathi told me you've been very diligent. So…" He shuffled the boxes and unhooked a cooler bag from his shoulder. "Drinks are on me."

Edwyn grabbed two bottles of cold beer and came over to sit by me. I ignored him and stared at Precious, who had turned her back on Tristan and sat facing the wall. The anger pouring off her was palpable and her way of dealing with it made me smile. She hadn't spoken to Tristan all week, despite numerous apologies about stealing our clothes.

Albert looked around bemused and tugged at his tie before unboxing the pizzas. "Is something going on?" Albert asked as he lifted the lid on the final box.

"No," Edwyn said. So that was how he was planning to play this.

I bided my time, working my way through a couple of pizza slices until Edwyn went for a bathroom break.

"Albert, can I talk to you for a minute? In private?"

"Of course." He led me to the hall and waited, giving me a kind smile. "What's the matter?"

I swallowed. "There was an incident while you were away."

"Oh?"

"On the physical asset check." I shoved the form at him. He read it without giving anything away.

"I see." Maybe I hadn't been descriptive enough when I described my experience, but it was hard when the form was clear it only wanted facts about injury.

"I almost died."

"This is very serious. How are you feeling in yourself now?"

"Better."

"Did you get medical attention?"

"No."

Edwyn paled as he walked back in. Crap. He knew I was telling on him.

"We shall remedy that straight away. I will ask Skathi to get his healers to check you over. Do you want to take a day at home? The portal's not due to open yet, but I can ask–"

"I'm alright." I didn't want a sick day blemishing my perfect attendance record.

"If you're sure. And I see Precious was the one who found you and performed CPR. I shall have to make sure we do something for Precious' quick thinking to apply chest compressions. I imagine it was traumatic. We have counselling available for any trauma or emotional damage you may wish to work through. I'll email you the number."

"Thank you." At last, someone was taking this seriously.

"And I'll remind my more experienced team members about the duty of care they have to our junior members of staff." He glared at Edwyn before patting my arm like a kindly uncle. "Look, auditing isn't for the faint of heart. It's a tough gig and there are more accidents than we'd care to admit. That's why we have such strict health and safety reporting processes and I'm sorry we let you down this time. It seems like this experience has affected you deeply, so I strongly recommend you take advantage of the professional counselling benefit – there's no cost to you and it's completely confidential."

I nodded.

"Do you need any time off? I'm sure we can handle the rest of the audit without you."

Take me off the audit? "No!" I almost shouted it.

"Alright, then." When I didn't move away, Albert asked, "Is

there anything else I can help with?"

My mouth opened and closed as he peered at me with that same benevolent, caring expression. "A fae stone is missing."

His forehead creased, and he tilted his head. "What do you mean?"

"I was in the water looking for a stone that had sunk, but it wasn't there. It had vanished."

"I see. Did anyone confirm this?" He held a hand up to forestall my protest. "It's not that I don't believe you, but we need to double check anything out of the ordinary."

"Precious. She can back me up."

"I see." He met my gaze and placed a thick hand on my shoulder. "Thank you for telling me. I'll look into it. Now, we'd better get back before they finish all the food."

He walked off and my shoulders dropped as some of the tension I'd held ebbed out of me. I had escalated the issue and done the right thing, and now it was out of my hands. Maybe I'd call the counselling hotline this weekend. But really, I just needed to relax and take a break and never go near the ocean again.

I couldn't wait for the week to finish so I could forget about work and have a night out with Abby.

Chapter 19

You don't have to be invited into the club to have a good time.

Club Blud's motto

"**I** cannot believe you almost got killed," Abby said for the fifth time as she applied blusher to my pale face.

"Audits are dangerous." I aimed for calm and casual. Judging by her look, I didn't pull it off. I shouldn't have told her about the sea monster, but she was my best friend, and she had a way of listening that pulled out everything, even things that shouldn't be shared because of certain non-disclosure clauses in my contract. But my contract hadn't said anything specific about sea monsters, so…

"How many graduates do you know who die on the job?" Darn her trying to use logic.

I reached for my phone. Abby slammed her hand over mine,

sending a fine dusting of pink powder over the desk. "Don't search it. It'll only make me worry about you more."

"Worrying is meant to be my thing." I gave her a weak smile.

"Are you going to call the counselling service at least?"

I shouldn't have told her about that either. "I don't need counselling." My gaze skittered around her bedroom. I wanted to do anything apart from meet her eyes.

The last time I'd been to a therapist had been a waste of time. Sure, the woman had been very understanding; she'd nodded sympathetically in all the right places before saying that she didn't think I had OCD and my compulsions were anxiety manifesting itself in behaviours. I'd been ten and didn't need a degree in psychology or whatever she had hanging on her whitewashed walls to know that. She'd given me some breathing exercises and told me to focus on the task at hand rather than the anxious thoughts that crowded my brain. Easier said than done.

And then the funding had run out. Or maybe it was because I moved families again. Whatever reason, the therapy sessions stopped, and I wasn't any better. So I'd learned to succeed despite my crazy and I *was* succeeding; I had the job I wanted and I was living my best life in a London flat. My gaze caught on the weird stain on her wall. Best life, I reminded myself as I checked my watch. Seven times.

"I think you should call," Abby said again.

"OK, maybe I'll call this weekend, but not tonight, OK? I've had a hard week and I've been looking forward to relaxing with you, getting distracted from work. Please?" I put on my begging face.

"Fine." Abby stuck out her bottom lip in a way that I knew meant she wouldn't drop this. She was an online agony aunt who believed in talking things through.

"So, I was thinking we could find a pool bar. There's one not too far that looks good." I showed her the pre-saved search on my phone.

Abby looked at it for all of ten seconds before shaking her head. "Hustling old men at some dodgy Conservative Club is not a distraction. I know just what you need…"

~

I pulled a face at the neon sign showing a red drop of blood inside a triangle as Abby flashed my work pass at the bouncer.

"Hey!" I snatched it back. When had she taken that?

She gave me an apologetic shrug then smirked as the bouncer let us in. Abby waved at the queue of people lining the street who didn't have a yellow lanyard to wave at the doorman.

Inside the glossy black door, the club assaulted all my senses apart from sight because it was so dark that I couldn't make out much more than the copper-coated bar at the back of the large room and a crush of bodies between us and it. But the noise and smell more than made up for the lack of sight.

Low, pulsating music surrounded us, cajoling my hips into moving to the beat while the heady scent of too much perfume and overpriced aftershave mixed with sweat engulfed my nostrils.

"Isn't this great?" Abby beamed at me.

I gave her a weak thumbs up.

"Let's get a drink." She grabbed my hand and pulled me through the press of dancing bodies.

Why couldn't we have gone to a pool bar?

Chapter 20

We are a family at the Bathory Corporation. I won't insult you by pretending that we're a happy family – we have our disagreements, of course, any family does. But we are all on the same side and if you mess with one of us, you mess with all of us.

Elizabeth Bathory – *Interview on the Phil Good show*

I crashed into the wall of the bar as the vampire pressed his body to mine. My breath left my lungs, and I squeaked at the unexpected attack.

"Mmmm, you smell good. I love that perfume…" His tongue ran up my neck.

I froze at the shock of his touch. Was this what passed as foreplay in London? My mind was unable to process the assault and focused on little details. My heart pounding in my ears. The slimy feel of his tongue on my skin, the striped pattern on his shirt – which was unbuttoned to an indecent low that exposed far too much of his chest, and the musky smell.

"I love that dress on you. You shouldn't wear it out though, it makes me want to do naughty things to you…" He trailed off, kissing my skin. "Remember last time when we…"

His words managed to penetrate my shock. I wore my flatmate's little black dress. In the darkness, he obviously thought I was her. I moved my hands until they were flat on his chest, ready to push him away and explain.

Pointed teeth grazed my neck, and my body froze again.

"Let's get this pesky lanyard out of the way…" He stopped and pulled back. "Holy dzrak." The Dwarfish curse word sounded strange in his mouth. "I didn't know you worked for Bathory. Why didn't you say something last time? Her employees are off limits." He stepped away from me and ran a hand through his jaw-length hair, his eyes darting around like my employers might lurk in the corners of the nightclub. "I could get into trouble for this."

Like it was my fault he'd decided to use me like a chew toy. Anger surged through my veins, and I found my voice. "I'm not Abby."

His gaze locked on my face. "You're not. But you smell like her and that dress…"

"We're flatmates." I cursed myself. I didn't owe him an explanation. He'd attacked me. It wasn't my fault I'd borrowed her dress and perfume for tonight. Why had I agreed to come to this stupid vampire club anyway? Next time we went out, I was insisting on going to a nice, cozy pool hall with better lighting.

"Oh. Cool. Is she here?" He scanned the room, looking for my flatmate.

"Like I'd tell you."

"So she is here. Tell her I'm up for round two if she is. And maybe don't wear her clothes."

"Maybe don't attack random women," I spat back at him.

He shrugged and walked to the bar.

I rubbed my neck, my hand clutching the scratchy lanyard that hung there. The Bathory Corporation had unknowingly saved me from a bite. It was ironic, given that new employees were juice boxes for the longer serving vampires that worked there.

With a shudder, I headed back to our table.

"You were gone a while. I ordered you another drink." Abby passed me a red cocktail.

I took a sip. It was too sweet, but maybe sugar was what I needed to calm the adrenaline spiking through my body. Why had I let her talk me into a night out? I downed the rest of the drink. "Tell me again why we came to this vampire bar?"

"What happened?" Her eyes filled with concern.

"A vampire mistook me for you."

Her eyebrows raised.

"I think he works here. He seemed to know you. Intimately."

She scratched her cheek before recognition flickered through her eyes. "Oh, him. He was fun, but not the best. You

OK?"

"Yeah. But I'd better head home. Work stuff." My job was taking over my life, nights out with friends included. I needed somewhere where I didn't have to worry about bloody vampires assaulting me.

She grabbed her bag.

"You can stay."

"Nah. This place is passé," Abby grinned at me. "Just let me go to the bathroom."

I smiled back, grateful for the camaraderie. Ever since I'd got this job, it had felt like a fight to fit in, a fight to do well. I was a kitten in with a bunch of tigers and I needed to sharpen my claws.

Chapter 21

Wigan Wonder does it again! Willa Wigglesby from Wigan wins local Rubik's cube contest, beating off fierce competition from the other twenty challengers. The cube master beat his previous personal best, but was half a second shy of the county record.

Wigan Weekly Gazette

I agreed to meet her outside and weaved my way through the bar, the loud music pulsing through my head, making it pound. This was not how I wanted my night of freedom to go.

Someone crashed into me. Still shaking from the assault, I shrank back.

"Sorry...Elle?" Strong arms gripped my shoulders. I whimpered even as I looked up into Liam's concerned face. I hadn't seen him since he'd fixed the laptop battery and his kind, concerned face brought tears to my eyes. "Come on, let's get some fresh air." He shifted one hand to my lower back and guided us through the crowd to the door.

Every time a vampire got too close to us, I flinched again. I needed to woman up, because I had to work with these creatures, and I couldn't spend my time in the office recoiling from all my colleagues. My attacker was an individual, not representative of the entire species. I mean, sure, my colleagues were mostly dicks, but that applied to the humans I worked with, too. And the vampires at work didn't push themselves on me like they wanted to…I felt hot tears welling up again.

He waved at a group of people sat in a booth as we passed. Most of them smiled back, but a gorgeous woman with the best hair I'd ever seen narrowed her eyes as we went, and she downed her martini. She wriggled onto a large man's lap and continued to stare daggers at us as we left.

I looked away and concentrated on putting one foot in front of the other and remembering to breathe. I tapped my fingers against my thigh. It was stupid, I knew, but it gave me some measure of control, as if tapping could stop bad things from happening. The cool night air washed over me like a welcome wave as we exited the club.

I closed my eyes and leaned against the wall. My hands trembled. Wait it wasn't just my hands; my entire body shook from the shock or maybe the beat from the music that pulsed through the bricks behind me. I desperately wanted to believe it was the beat.

"What happened?" Liam asked in his calm, low voice.

I looked up at him and shook my head. I couldn't verbalise it. I'd had the worse week of my life; almost killed by a sea monster, Tristan had hung my clothes out so the world could see my spare underwear, and now I'd been assaulted by a vampire.

He must have seen something of my trauma written on my face because he pulled me into a hug. Not a soft 'I'm sorry, but this is nothing to do with me' hug, but a tight embrace that I could almost believe meant he wanted to share my pain.

Tears pooled in my eyes before spilling over. Crap. Now I was getting his shirt wet. I pulled back, but he crushed me to him, allowing me to lose it in the steady unyielding comfort of his arms. I let myself fall into it, closing my eyes and sinking into the reassuring hug, his body warm against my cool skin, until I felt a little better.

"Do you need a Rubik's cube?" Liam asked into my hair.

I managed a laugh as I pulled back, and this time he let me go. I sniffed as I cracked my eyes open and drank him in. His tone had been light, but his dark brown eyes were filled with concern and he looked extra handsome in a fitted navy-blue shirt – oh crap, there was a hideous dark patch where I'd cried on him. My gaze trailed down to where his sleeves were rolled up to his elbows, revealing toned forearms. Why did rolled up sleeves make guys look hotter? That was one of the mysteries of the universe.

I fought back a giggle at my own stupid thoughts – I'd just been assaulted and now I was eyeing up the IT guy. What was wrong with me? I tore my gaze away from those toned forearms. "Do you carry a cube around with you everywhere?" I asked.

With a sheepish grin, he pulled a keyring out of his pocket. And, yes, there was a miniature pyramid version of a Rubik's cube attached to it. I laughed and held out my hand. He'd saved the day again. With something to occupy my hands, I relaxed. Solving the puzzle was something I could do, and it helped calm my mind more than the tapping ever could. As I worked through the motions, I realised why he looked different in the club. "You're not wearing your glasses," I blurted out.

He rubbed at his eyes. "Rani prefers me in contacts, but they make my eyeballs itch." He shrugged like he accepted he should give up his comfort for someone else.

"I like your glasses." I clamped my mouth shut. Why did my voice work before my brain? I blame the alcohol and the vampires.

"Thanks," Liam said with a grin that made my breath catch. He didn't notice. "You ever think of entering tournaments?" he asked, his attention back on the Rubik's cube in my hand.

I shook my head. "I'm not that good."

"I entered one once."

"Really?" I tore my gaze from the pyramid and my fingers paused in twisting the pieces.

"Got my arse handed to me by a ten-year-old from Wigan." I snorted.

His eyes glinted in the red light from the nightclub's sign.

"You should laugh more often."

"How do you know I don't laugh all the time?"

"You work at the Bathory Corporation. There aren't many laughs there."

"Sure there are, audit's a gas," I deadpanned.

"Yeah, laugh a minute, I bet."

"You should see some of the record keeping."

"Almost as fun as being in IT," he replied.

"I hear you can't be Siri-ous with all that tech around you." It was an awful pun. We didn't even use Apple macs at work.

"At least we've got all the food we can eat…if you like microchips."

We looked at each other before laughing out loud. This time the tears I wiped from my eyes were from mirth. It was a welcome release of everything; the nervous tension I'd carried around with me, the horror of the attack, the dread of getting fed on by my colleagues. Sometimes all you needed was a good laugh. Much better medicine than facing my problems like Abby wanted me to do.

Once we could breathe again, Liam nudged me with his shoulder. The warm touch felt good, especially when he didn't move away and our arms stayed connected. It felt intimate, like we shared a secret. "Do you want to talk about whatever you were running away from in there?"

"Just some asshole vampire and a case of mistaken identity."

"Yeah, they're absolute dzrakers alright."

"I'll drink to that." I raised the pyramid as if it was a glass. "You know," I mused, the alcohol in my system making me talkative, "the concept of absolute dzrakers, means there must be a base from which all dzrakers are judged, and it implies the existence of negative dzrakers…"

"Like a nice person?" Liam frowned in confusion at my maths logic.

"Like you." *Crap.* Why had I said that?

"Do you want to go back inside, or can I see you home?"

"I don't think your friends would be happy if you walked out on them."

"It's OK, this," he gestured at the club, "isn't really my scene but Rani wanted to come, and I tend to do whatever she wants." He gave me a sad smile. "Makes my life easier."

My body had turned cold the second he'd mentioned the woman's name. The glowering girl in the booth now made sense. But he hadn't said she was his girlfriend. Maybe they were just friends.

"So, do you want me to take you home?" Liam's voice was low, and his eyes were soft.

I shivered at his words. I wanted more than anything for him to take me home and…

"Elle?" Abby's voice poured cold water over whatever fantasy my tired brain concocted. "Are you ready to go?" She stopped short, her gaze raking over Liam. A flash of anger heated me. I shook it away. He wasn't mine. She had every right to look at him. I was probably experiencing after-drinks hanger – hungry anger – and needed some late-night chips to calm me down. Oblivious of my need for carbs, Abby purred, "Who's this?"

"This is Liam. He works in IT."

"Does he?"

"I do," Liam said, shaking her hand. "Elle looked upset, so I've been keeping her company."

"Thank you. It's nice to know she's got people at her work who care about her."

What did that mean?

"Us low-level employees need to look after each other." He shot me a grin.

What did *that* mean? He'd been working there for longer than me and he had a permanent job in IT. He wasn't low level. Except he worked in the basement. But the senior vampires had their offices in the basement. My head hurt.

Liam held out his hand to me. Confused, I shook it. Bit of a formal way to end the evening, but OK. He bit his lip, shoulders rocking as he suppressed a laugh. "My keys?"

"Oh, right." I still had his keyring. And I shouldn't steal a second Rubik's puzzle off him. I handed them back, hoping it was too dark for him to see the blush that flamed my cheeks.

"See you around, Elle."

"See you around." I watched him walk back inside and was proud that I didn't notice how well his jeans fit. Not much, anyway.

"You never mentioned you worked with that hottie? Anything you want to tell me?"

"He's just someone I work with." Because there wasn't anything there. I'd misread kindness for attraction, and I was tipsy. I needed to get some sleep and forget this night had ever happened.

Chapter 22

A free counselling service is available to all employees.

Bathory Corporation Employee Handbook

I awoke in a flush of sweat, fighting off my covers before realising I was in bed. Safe. There was no attacker cornering me in a dark club corner, no monster tugging me to the depths. Safe.

Nibbles gave me a concerned squeak from his cage in the corner of my room.

"It's alright, I'm alright." I petted him, letting his long fur soothe me. "Ouch!" I had stroked him for more than the five pets he allotted before he got bitey. "Just for that, you can wait for your treats until after I've got a plaster."

I made my way to the shared bathroom, found a plaster and grimaced at the mirror. I was so pale, I looked grey with dark smudges under my eyes and lank hair. I needed a shower. Nibbles would have to wait a bit longer.

Once I was clean, and looked almost human, I padded back to my room and fed my giant guinea-pig sized hamster his seed treats. "Do you think I should call the counselling service?" I asked him.

He looked up at me with his bulging brownish-red eyes and squeaked. Was that a yes? Then he swiped the treat from my hand and scurried back into his bed, sending shredded paper flying as he burrowed in.

I got dressed slowly and made my decision. I would call the counselling line…after I'd cleaned the flat. "And I'm starting with your cage," I said to Nibbles.

~

I banged the slow cooker that we never used back into the cupboard. OK, that was the kitchen done, as well as my bedroom, the lounge area, and a thorough clean of my gigantic hamster's cage, which he had shown his appreciation for by taking a crap in the middle of my room while I cleared out his bedding.

Bathroom next.

"Elle!" Abby screeched from her doorway. Her purple satin eye mask sat on her forehead, and she had her hands on her hips, bunching up the silk of her nightdress. Even sleeping, she had a level of elegance that I couldn't match. "What are you doing?"

"Cleaning," I said guiltily.

"At eight o' clock in the morning? On a Saturday?"

I checked my watch, smiling at the Lilo and Stitch motif on the face. "It's eleven o'clock."

That took the wind out of her sails. She stomped back in to check her phone before storming out. "It's still Saturday. Hang on," she screwed up her lips and narrowed her eyes, "why are you cleaning?"

"I just like a tidy flat." Everything was better when it was clean. "I think I'll check the smoke alarm batteries…"

"No. This isn't your normal level of cleaning…" she glanced at the grout cleaner I had out on the side, "this is stress cleaning." Her voice softened, "Because of what happened?"

I opened my mouth to say something, but she kept on talking.

"No," she shook her head, "not that." Abby clicked her fingers. "You're avoiding something. Wait, did something happen with Liam?"

"No!"

"OK, let me think…you're keeping busy so you don't have to call the counsellor, aren't you?"

My guilty face must have given something away.

"I knew it! Stop procrastinating, get back in your room and call them. You promised me."

Turning on the guilt trip worked. I squirmed under her hard

stare. "I will call them…after I've done the bathroom."

"You can do the bathroom after you've called them because I am going in now and I'm going to have a nice long bath with the special bubble bath, and I don't want to hear any cleaning or banging for at least an hour. Understood." She didn't give me a chance to answer as she stormed into the bathroom.

A rebellious streak inside me made me clean the skirting boards, but then I was truly out of things to do. I had better make that call.

~

The phone rang. Maybe they didn't work weekends. Maybe this was a sign from the universe that I shouldn't call. I could suck it up and bury the anxiety deep down. What harm could that do?

Harm. I had to prevent harm. To everyone. As if on cue, my hand started tapping the side of my bed, convinced that I just had to beat out a certain rhythm so many times and everything would be alright. If only it worked like that.

Nibbles squeaked at me. He was right; I needed to make this call. I clung to my phone until someone picked up. It had only taken five rings, but it felt like an eternity.

"Good morning, this is the Bathory Corporation counselling

service," said a neutral voice on the other end of the phone. "May I have your employee ID number?"

"I thought this was a confidential service." My heart raced. What if Albert heard I'd called? Would he be glad I'd taken him up on his suggestion or annoyed that I'd revealed the lapse of duty of care in his team.

"That's correct," the voice replied. I couldn't tell if they were male or female. "Nothing you tell us will be shared with your company, but we need to make sure you actually work for the corporation."

"People really call up when they don't work there?"

"You'd be surprised."

I reeled off the set of numbers I'd memorised when I'd joined.

"Great. My name is Jesse," I still had no clue if that was a male or female name. Maybe it didn't matter. "What would you like me to call you?"

"Don't you already know my name from my employee number?"

"It comes up with a pass or fail on whether the ID is genuine. I don't have any more details, but I find it helps to have a name."

"Call me Abby." It was petty, I knew, but I was still annoyed that Abby had made me call.

"Alright, Abby. How can I help you today?"

I sucked in a deep breath. This was it. My voice stuck in my throat. I made a choking sound. Why couldn't I get it out.

Jesse stayed silent, waiting for me to speak first in a classic therapist move.

Eventually, I squeaked out, "I've had a really bad week." That was an understatement.

"Everyone has bad weeks sometimes. Would you like to share a bit more about what made this week so bad?"

"A vampire attacked me." I'd build up to the sea monster.

"I see. And did they take more than the allotted amount of blood?"

"No." I shook my head even though they couldn't see me. "It wasn't at work."

"Ah. But it's affecting your work."

"I don't know. It happened on Friday night."

"I see. Well, it's important to remember that within the corporation, everyone is bound by a code of conduct."

"I don't think they work for the company."

"I see." That seemed to be Jesse's catch phrase. "The Bathory Corporation isn't responsible for the conduct of all vampires. But if it helps, I can email you a pamphlet about disassociating the behaviour of other vampires with the ones who work for the company."

"I don't want a leaflet. Aren't you meant to ask me how it made me feel?" I'd been to counselling before; I knew how it went. A horrible hour spent analysing emotions and my failure at controlling my compulsions.

"How did it make you feel?" asked Jesse.

"Angry." Huh. I pondered on that. "Really angry. I shouldn't have to deal with getting assaulted when I'm out having fun with my friends."

"No one should have to deal with that."

"Damn right. I should have reported him." Maybe I would. Abby must have his name if they'd hooked up. Well, she might have his name.

"Action is always a positive step to taking back control," said Jesse in a soothing voice.

"I can take action with the vampire, but what about the sea monster?"

There was a long pause. "Sea monster?"

Right. I hadn't told them that story yet. "That's the other reason I wanted to call. I got attacked by a sea monster at work and almost died."

Jesse gave a low whistle. "Well, that is a new one. I've been doing this for two years and I don't think I've heard about a sea monster before. Not since Triton left, anyway."

"Glad I could make your day more interesting." I laced my voice with sarcasm.

"Oh." They settled back into a soothing tone. "And how did that make you feel?"

"Small. Terrified." My hand went to my leg where welts still stuck out from the creature's poisoned tentacles. My lip wobbled. I could feel the searing water pouring into my lungs, cutting off my oxygen. I had felt powerless.

"That's understandable. It can be hard to feel like you're not in control."

"It's more than that. I shouldn't have been put into the position in the first place. I'm a graduate, not a scuba diver."

"You sound angry, Abby."

"Yeah. I *am* angry. I shouldn't have to feel like my life is in danger on the job."

"There are rules and clauses in your contract designed to protect you," Jesse agreed. "Do you feel like any of these were broken?"

"I don't know."

"Which department do you work in?"

"Fae audits." I said it without thinking. Crap. Now I was less anonymous. At least they didn't know my real name.

Jesse gave another tuneless whistle. "Wow. You're in at the deep end, there. Oops, pardon the pun."

This was nothing like the counselling I'd had during my teens. "Aren't you meant to help me?" I asked.

"Right. Do you want to talk about it?"

I drew my knees up to my chest and hugged them with my free arm. "No."

"Did you complete an incident report?"

"Yes. My boss did that with me."

"Good. So how would you like me to help you?"

"I don't know."

Jesse waited a beat before sighing. "OK, look, your contract has the usual clauses about loss of life and danger, especially in Fae Audits, but it also has a standard notice period. You don't have to stay."

"You think I should quit?"

"I don't think anything. I'm a counsellor, that's all. I'm giving you options. And reminding you that you always have choices."

Choices. I mulled over the word. What choices did I have?

Jesse carried on. "When we feel powerless and small, it's often because we feel like our agency has been removed, that we don't have choices. You have some."

"But–"

"You might not like them, but you always have a choice. In this case, the extreme option could be to leave."

"Do you think I should leave?"

"That's not my decision to make."

Damn, Jesse might actually be a good counsellor. "If you were me, what would you do?"

"I can't answer that. But you are you, what are you going to do?"

My choices whirled around my head. Stay or go. Just like in that song that came on the radio every now and then. "I'm going to make a list of pros and cons. Thanks Jesse, you've been really helpful." I hung up and pulled out my notebook to make my list.

Pro: This was my dream job. I added a star next to that one because it had to count for more.

Con: I'd nearly gotten killed. I drew a star next to that too.

Pro: I was still alive.

Con: The people I worked with were horrible. But not all of them. Precious was great. I added her name to the pro column.

After fifteen more minutes, the con column was considerably larger than the pro list. I tapped my pen against the lined paper. But if I let a long list of cons stop me, I'd never have gone to university or applied for the graduate scheme in the first place. And why did my gut twist at the thought of leaving?

This was the first step to my dream of becoming a director by the time I was thirty at the best company in the UK. I wouldn't get another opportunity like this. My resolve stiffened. I would stay. And I would show everyone who doubted me that Elle Bruma was a force to be reckoned with.

Besides, I could always choose to leave later.

Chapter 23

It's important to foster a culture of camaraderie within a team. It makes everyone strive harder to achieve the collective goal.

Elizabeth Bathory – *The First Disrupter*

Monday morning rolled around, and I was up and ready before the crack of dawn, determined to beat Tristan to the office. This was a good week. I could feel it in my bones. The physical asset test had finished, so there was minimal risk of death this week. I said goodbye to Nibbles, left a note for Abby and headed to the office with a skip in my step.

The bounce left me as soon as I saw Tristan's laptop at his desk. He must have left it here at the weekend. Sneaky so and so.

As if my thoughts summoned him, he pranced into the office, hair wet, and stared at me. "What are you doing here?"

"I could ask you the same question. Why is your hair wet?"

"Shower." He heaved a sigh at my puzzled look and explained, "On Sunday nights, I come to the office, sleep in the infirmary bed, shower in the gym and get to my desk before anyone else. Looking dedicated and impressing the bosses."

"We have a gym?"

"Are you going to tell anyone?"

I sighed. "Your secret's safe with me." I couldn't decide if his plan was ingenious or way too much effort to be the first one in the office. "Besides, it only works with a human boss."

"What?"

"Vampires work at night." I tilted my head towards a vampire tapping away at their laptop in the opposite corner to us. "What are you going to do when you change department?"

He gave me a long look. "Haven't you got work to do?"

I allowed myself a small smile and turned on the laptop. My email inbox had filled up again and I went to work clearing it. One made me pause. Newton had messaged about our first mentoring meeting. Next Friday night at eight p.m. I replied saying that, of course, I'd make it and put the meeting in the diary.

Fred made his way over to our bank of desks. "Thanks for the viewing tip – the Office. It's bloody brilliant. Hilarious." He shook his head. "I can't believe I haven't seen it before. I haven't laughed that much since Monty Python."

"Oh, yah. And you really do look like him."

The vampire broke into a strange dance, while making a strange noise that might have been a song.

"Good one." Tristan gave him a high five.

"What was that meant to be?" I asked.

"The dance, from the Office, you know."

They both started making odd, offbeat dance moves while humming an offkey tune. I stared at them. It was too early in the morning for this crap.

Precious came in, stifling a yawn and stopped dead in the doorway. "I'm still asleep and this is a nightmare."

"Come on, Presh, dance with us." Tristan shimmied over to her.

She shrugged off her laptop bag and ignored Tristan as she slumped into a free chair. Edwyn was next, clutching a coffee cup. He jerked back as the vampire's arm swung in his direction, spilling his drink on the floor. "What fresh hell is this?"

"Just doing a bit of dancing. Catch you later." The vampire grinned and left, leaving Edwyn glaring after him.

"I'm getting a top-up." He turned and bumped into Albert, who burst through the door.

"No time for a coffee run." Albert beamed at us. "Nice to see you all bright and early, team. Let's go." Albert headed out and Tristan scrabbled to be the first after him. Precious rolled her eyes at me and followed.

Edwyn hung back and leaned on my desk as I packed up my

computer. "I cannot believe you told Albert."

"I couldn't hide the incident report. And the employee handbook says–"

"I was going to tell him myself. In person. Now he thinks I'm keeping things from him."

I felt a twinge of sympathy, but I crushed it. He hadn't gotten me medical attention, he hadn't reported Tristan for stealing our clothes. His apology was half-assed at best. I shrugged.

He invaded my personal space, and my breathing ratcheted up as he stared down at me. "I don't know what game you think you're playing, but you are not messing up my promotion. So, from now on, you listen to me, and you do what I tell you, or we're going to have a problem. Capiche?"

I nodded, and he left me standing in the office, breathing hard. If he hadn't looked so menacing, I could have laughed at his use of outdated mafia slang. It was cutthroat here. If I hadn't realised it before, Edwyn's reaction confirmed it. I swallowed and hurried after the rest of the team, entering Pytha's domain in time to hear her purr at Edwyn.

"What have you brought me today?" she asked, her gaze firmly on Edwyn.

He winced. "I forgot the chocolates."

"Then why do I smell something sweet?"

"It's the caramel in my latte."

She ran her tongue over her top lip and held out her hand. Edwyn clung to his half-empty coffee cup, but at a nod from Albert, he handed it over. His fingers lingered on the cup, as if it was the most precious thing in the world, and a flicker of sadness and longing sped across his features. Pytha's fingers touched his as she accepted the cup and he jerked back with enough force that a spoonful of the remaining coffee sloshed out of the cup, down the side and over her hand.

Pytha kept her eyes on Edwyn as she swapped her hands over and inserted one wet finger into her mouth, licking it seductively as she smiled. He looked away and I heard Precious murmur, "Damn, that is hot," behind me.

"Delicious." Pytha licked her lips again, looking Edwyn up and down, before resting the cup on her living table and summoning the portal.

On the other side, Albert thrust his briefcase at Edwyn. "I don't know what's got into you, Winnie. You don't report an incident and now you've forgotten the chocolates. I thought you were ready for a senior management position, but it looks like I was mistaken."

I shared a look with Precious and mouthed, "Winnie?"

She raised her eyebrows at me as Edwyn hung his head. Once Albert was out of earshot, he turned on us. "Get a move on."

Precious gave him a mock salute. "Aye, aye, Winnie."

He scowled, shoved his suitcase at Tristan, and headed after Albert. We burst into laughter and followed on.

Chapter 24

It's important to have a mentor, someone who can provide advice and guidance, someone who can support you as you develop your career. A good mentor can be the difference between corporate success or failure.

Elizabeth Bathory – *The First Disrupter*

I was right to be wary of Edwyn. He'd spent the week taking out Albert's disappointment on me. I was relegated to tea duty and given the oldest, most indecipherable contracts to work through. I'd started a database of names, locations and frequent terms, but it was hard work and my head throbbed. He'd given me extra paperwork while the others tromped round the island to repeat part of the physical assets test for reasons I guessed boiled down to he was pissed. And now, thanks to the extra work, I was behind with my studies too.

All I wanted was to go home and enjoy a couple of days of

rest before starting again. But, thanks to Edwyn's vindictiveness, he'd asked me to cart several boxes through the portal and take them up to the office so we could sort through them over the weekend and save some time on the audit. Time we wouldn't need to save if he hadn't insisted on a full asset test. And by we, he meant us grads. By the time I'd lugged all four boxes upstairs, it was five past eight.

My deskphone rang. It took me a second to work out it was my phone as no one had called me before. I answered it.

"You are late, Miss Bruma." Newton's voice sounded through the speaker.

"What?"

"For our mentor meeting. It started at eight p.m. and it is now five past."

"No, we don't have a meeting today. It's next week." I scrambled to find my schedule.

"I moved it forward."

Crap. There it was. Debbie must have accepted the invite without checking with me. "Sorry, I had to finish carting these boxes around–" My gaze sought out her dark head as she tapped away at the keyboard.

"Spare me your excuses and get here." He hung up with a click.

I groaned and grabbed my bag. On my way to the lift, I stopped at Debbie's desk.

She looked up with a questioning expression on her face. "Can I help you?"

"Did you put a meeting with my mentor in my diary?" At her slight puzzlement, I added, "Mr Newton."

"Oh, yes, I believe I did." She checked the time and her eyes widened. "I believe it started a few minutes ago, you should get going." There was a hint of innocence to her voice.

I felt bad talking to her about this, but I had to make my point. This was part of the new, more confident, Elle. "Yes, next time, can you let me know before you change any appointments?"

"It was in your calendar."

"Yes, but I didn't get any alerts."

"How frustrating." Did the corner of her lip curl into a smirk? Her eyes glowed for an instant under the electric lights.

I shook my head. Now I was seeing things.

"I'll try harder next time," Debbie said, her bland smile settling back over her features.

"Thanks," I replied before dashing for the lift. I should feel good; I had made my point, she had sympathised with me, but I got the same nagging sense of frustration as before. I adjusted the strap on my bag. *Breathe, Elle, focus on the mentor meeting.*

I managed to find the meeting room – unusually for a senior vampire, he didn't have an office in the basement – and threw open the door, panting.

Newton finished writing something in a leatherbound book and regarded me with his head tilted slightly to the side. "I am a very busy man, Miss Bruma, and I expect you to be punctual for all of our meetings. Do I make myself clear?"

"Yes, sir. It won't happen again."

"Good." He studied me for a moment longer. I squirmed on my chair, feeling like a mouse being eyed by a cat, and averted my gaze, taking in his office. A large model of an eyeball sat on top of a wooden cabinet next to a brass astrolabe in a stand. Maps and astrological prints filled one side of the room while a chalkboard covered in writing lined the opposite wall. Planets hung from the ceiling, moving slowly in rotation as I watched. It looked more like a professor's study than an executive office.

"Are you quite well?"

"Huh? I mean, yes, sir."

"Then perhaps you could sit still instead of twitching your legs like you want to run out of here."

My eyes lifted to meet his gaze. I thought I saw the ghost of a smile pass over his lips before it was gone. I ground my heels into the plush carpet that covered his office floor and gripped my notepad to stop my hands twitching.

"Have you chosen the qualification you want to study?"

"Yes, accounting. I think it fits well with my placement and future ambitions. My first exams are booked for December."

"It will be useful, yes. And how are your studies going?"

"It's difficult to fit it in with work…"

"No one said it wouldn't be."

"…but I'm managing." So far, I'd managed to study a little each night and there was still plenty of time before the exams. The sums were easy enough; it was all the accounting regulations and samples of case law to remember that caused my head to ache.

"I'm glad to hear it. So, how is your first placement?"

"Good."

He raised one eyebrow and stared at me. My gaze darted around his office, taking in the oil paintings on the wall and the smoked glass windows.

I let out a long sigh. How could I tell him? He waited, holding the silence until something cracked within me. "It's not going well. I almost died. And my manager hates me and Albert's disappointed in me and I'm behind on my studies and it's…it's not what I thought it would be here."

"I see."

I waited but he didn't say anything else. "So…what should I do?"

"If you dislike it so much here, then leave."

"What?"

"Quit. Hand in your notice. Go."

I stared at him, unsure if he was serious or not.

"We saw something in your assessment centre that made many of us think it was worth having you join the Corporation. Ahrens, in particular, was adamant that you would be a good fit, despite your…proclivity to nausea in public speaking. And I confess I was intrigued by how you responded to my compulsion to calm down. It's not often that someone can resist my mesmerisation…"

A flush flamed slowly up my neck. Newton's gaze flicked to my throat, no doubt his vampire senses picked up the increase in blood, but my rational mind couldn't stop the inexorable progress of my blush as it made its way to my cheeks and from there, it flooded out to my entire face.

"No one pretended it would be easy. In fact, Bathory made it quite clear in her introduction that there is a large percentage of graduates who do not make it past their first year. I have to say that I hoped you would, but no one is forcing you to be here." He stared at me again, capturing me with his red eyes. "So, if you do not wish to stay, leave."

There was an emphasis on the last word that made my heart race. He wanted me gone. I had failed. I swallowed hard, not knowing what to do. This was not how I thought my first mentor meeting would go. If I was honest with myself, I'd hoped for a meeting of the minds, sharing of advice and helpful anecdotes, perhaps over a coffee or tea, that would end with a genuine bond of friendship and mutual respect and an offer to come and speak with him whenever I needed a heart to heart. Instead, I got a cold vampire telling me to leave.

"In fact, why don't you leave through that window?" Newton's eyes shone red. A dizzy feeling flooded my brain for a moment, and I was halfway standing from my seat before I blinked it away.

"Did you say leave through the window?"

"Fascinating," he replied, jotting something down on a pad of yellow lined paper next to his laptop.

What had just happened? "So, I should just go?"

"You always have a choice. It's your choice, Elle, but I thought you were strong."

With that, he broke away and tapped at his laptop.

Just when I thought that was a dismissal, he spoke again. "Tell me, do you have any supernatural blood?"

I repressed a shudder. Were all vampires obsessed with blood? "No."

He raised an eyebrow.

"I don't know." The other eyebrow joined the first in silent question, and I continued, reciting the same sing song refrain I'd told people every time their questions turned to family. "I'm a foster kid, so I don't know who my parents are. Well, I know their names, but they died in a car accident when I was three, so I never met them. But, I don't think I'm supernatural. No magic, no powers. Nothing."

It would be so much easier if I was magical, then I'd be someone special, able to use my powers for good and I wouldn't need to fit in so much. I'd lost count of the times I'd wished for some sort of magic growing up, something that would mark me as different, as worthy of love, and, in my darkest times, something that would stop the bullies the next time they cornered me, or would let me fight back against the adults who terrified me.

"Hmmm." Newton's non-committal sound drew my

thoughts back to the present.

"Is being supernatural a pre-requisite to work here?" I felt I had to ask a question, anything to help me regain control of the situation.

"No, we're an equal opportunities employer. I was curious, that's all. It might explain your resistance, either that or your possess a unique strength of mind. Enjoy the rest of your day, Miss Bruma."

At his dismissal, I stuffed my notebook and pen into my bag and headed out of his office. My anxiety spiked. He had practically told me to quit, then changed the subject to supernaturals. I had no idea what any of it meant. I checked my bag for my keys, phone and wallet seven times as the elevator moved, and my stomach lurched. I needed to get home and destress, rearrange the kitchen cupboards, anything.

The doors slid open, and I took a step, almost bumping into someone. I apologised, rushed out, then realised I wasn't on the ground floor.

"Are you alright?"

I turned back and faced the knowing grin on Liam's face. Why was I always bumping into him? Couldn't I have one interaction with the man without looking like a complete klutz?

With a scowl, I got back into the lift, suddenly aware of what had happened; the elevator had gone down past the ground floor and, like a moron, I had barrelled out as soon as the doors opened. I got back in and stabbed at the already lit up

G button.

"Bad day?" he asked, still wearing that grin.

"You have no idea," I mumbled.

"Maybe I do." At his statement, I looked at him, really looked. Bags stretched out under his chocolate brown eyes, marring his face and lending him an air of world weariness that didn't sit well with the lower half of his face, that seemed ready to smile at the slightest provocation.

"So why not quit?" I echoed Newton's words to him and the left corner of the IT guy's mouth hooked up in a sardonic smile.

"Quit? I can't leave."

"Why not?"

He tilted his head on one side and took me in. "Where else would I go? Besides, once you've been here longer than two years, they've got you."

I frowned.

"Didn't they tell you? More than two years and you're a lifer. Here for life."

"Is that why you're here?"

He laughed. "No, I'm cursed. That's why I'm here."

I smiled along. He was strange, but I liked his sense of humour, he reminded me of some of the people I'd studied with. If he cracked out a maths joke, we'd be friends for life. "Maybe I'm cursed too."

"Then I look forward to working with you." He pushed his

glasses up on the bridge of his nose and made his voice deep and spooky as he added, "For the rest of your life."

There was nothing I could say to that, so I changed the topic. "You're wearing your glasses again."

Liam rubbed at his eyes. "Yeah, I got an infection from the contact lenses."

"I prefer them," I said with a shy smile, glad he'd stood up to his friend who'd wanted to change him.

"Me too."

My stomach turned. Was this a moment? It felt like we'd shared something intimate, but we'd just joked about work, and I'd complimented his glasses. What should I do now? Abby would have a witty reply, Precious would say exactly what she wanted, but I kept quiet and studied the carpeted floor.

The lift came to a smooth stop, and he gestured for me to step out first. We walked across the atrium together in silence and his words echoed round my head in time with my steps. Here for life.

We descended the steps outside and both of us paused on the pavement, the crisp night air rushing past in an autumn breeze that hinted at rain. A lone protestor stood off to one side, her jacket collar high against the chill.

"Do you know you're in league with the devil?" she asked, waving her painted cardboard sign at us.

"Really?" he laced his voice with mocking interest, and I covered my mouth to prevent a snort of laughter.

She nodded and moved a step closer. "Vampires, sired by the devil himself, luring innocent humans with the promise of riches."

"Not all humans are innocent," he said, an edge of darkness to his voice, the joking tone gone.

"Hey, leave her alone." I touched his arm, and he span back to me, whatever had troubled him still etched on his face, fierce and dangerous. The protestor mumbled something and moved back to her spot by the wall. Nervous, I removed my hand and shoved it into my jacket pocket, where I touched my fingers against my thumb, one by one. "So, I'm this way."

His face softened, and he was once again the slightly odd IT guy. He pushed his hands through his mop of straight black hair and smiled. "Ah, I'm over there."

A pause stretched between us. Should I ask him out? What if he said no? Confident Elle should say something. But the silence had gone on too long.

"Well, see you around," I said. *Idiot.*

With that, I left for the tube, annoyed with myself for not asking him for a drink as I battled the growing wind all the way to the station.

Chapter 25

Dedication to a purpose is something to be admired.

Elizabeth Bathory – *The First Disrupter*

I woke with a start and a couple of pages fell from where they'd been stuck to my face. Somewhere in the flat, my alarm blared.

"Turn that off," came Abby's voice from her room, followed by a low grumble. She must have got lucky last night. No surprise there. I was pretty sure she was on a mission to sleep with the entirety of London's young and single supernatural population.

I found my alarm and ended it before blinking down at the time. I was late. I shoved some food into Nibbles' cage, while pulling on trousers and a shirt, which ended in me falling to the ground, tangled in my own clothes.

Abby came out of her room, rubbing her eyes. "Are you OK? I heard a thud."

I buttoned my trousers, sat up and moved onto my shirt. "Fine. Just late. Must have slept through my first alarm."

"Wow, you must be tired if that was your backup."

My body answered for me with a yawn as I fastened the final button.

"You've done your buttons up wrong. Let me make you some coffee."

I stared down at my chest and rebuttoned my shirt. Abby waved away my protests and poured me a cup of coffee. Goblin Blend; the good stuff. The coffee we kept for special occasions like relatives' visits. Abby's relatives anyway, none of my foster carers stayed in touch. "Thought you could do with a strong coffee."

"Thanks." I took the travel mug gratefully and grabbed my pre-packed suitcase, turned back for my study notes and ran out of our apartment, not quickly enough to stop me getting a face full of hairy man chest as my flatmate's latest conquest stepped out of the bedroom wearing her dressing gown, which was too short and too open to hide anything.

With a squeak, I left and dashed for the tube, sanitising my hands and face with my travel bottle of hand sanitiser on the way. That chest hair was not hygienic. It was prime commuting time, which meant I had to fight for a spot on the platform before we all squeezed into an overcrowded capsule. Commuters glared at me as I hefted my small suitcase onto the train, taking up valuable floorspace. I apologised and wedged myself into a corner by the door, taking up as little space as possible.

At each station, more people crowded in, wearing suits and work gear, all sweating in their winter coats as the cramped train heated to the temperature of a tropical island, made humid from breath and sweat. Someone reached for the rail above my head and I spent the next hour staring at their armpit, trying not to breathe too deeply as a mixture of cologne and body odour threatened to choke me.

I tried to get my notes out and use the time for studying, but the slightest shift of my body had everyone in the packed space staring at me with barely controlled anger. Instead, I gazed at passing advertisements promising everything from weight loss to better bank accounts to sexy underwear and when the novelty of bright posters wore out, I focused on people's footwear.

It was an unwritten rule of the commute never to make eye contact. It made people nervous and you might accidentally meet the gaze of one of the crazy people who rode the tube, or worse, one of the men and women who wanted to convert you to their cult religion. I watched a pair of flip-flops tap out a beat in time with the loud music blaring over someone's headphones. A boot scratched its owner's calf. The points of a pair of winkle pickers got stuck under someone's heel and the man nearly fell when he tried to get off at Bank station.

And then, lulled by the rocking motion of the London underground, I closed my eyes and dozed. I awoke to the sound of a platform announcement, and it took me a precious second to realise it was my stop. I lifted my suitcase and pushed through with mumbled apologies.

The heavy sigh of doors closing told me I wasn't quick enough. In desperation, I flung my arm out, wincing as the doors bounced off it, but they didn't close. I squeezed through the gap and made it onto the crowded platform. Placing my suitcase on the concrete floor, I joined the press of people heading for the exit.

Out on the streets, I ran, then wheezed, then jogged, then walked to the Bathory Corporation building. It was half past eight. I had missed the portal. Ignoring the protestor, still waving her sign about the evils of the company, I dashed up the steps, my suitcase bouncing behind me and glugged my cooling coffee, scanning my pass in a jerky motion and then I was through.

My quick pace and squeaking suitcase wheel drew stares as I headed for Pytha's office. She wasn't there when I arrived. There was a strange sensation, like cobwebs or grass brushing over my skin. It lasted for a moment, before ebbing away. I stood, awkward in her space.

The plants leant their own exoticism to the room, and I swear a rhythmic breathing filled the air. A fern growing from a pot in the wall looked fuzzy. I reached out my hand to stroke it. It recoiled, curling in on itself to escape my touch.

The hazy light grew darker, and something snaked around my leg. I looked down and saw a grasping vine wrapping itself around me. I stamped on it with my other foot, but it wrapped around that one too, pulling tight so my legs were forced together. Panic filled my chest, and I fought for a breath as memories of another monster winding its tentacles around me clouded my mind.

I clawed at the vine, digging my nails into its thick shoot, but tendrils oozed around my hands, binding them. Unable to move my limbs, I shook my body as the trailing plant wrapped itself around me, turning me into some sort of weird mummy. I screamed.

"There's no need for that." Pytha's voice rang through the room, soft and full of the promise of spring. "Why are you breaking into my office?"

"I didn't break in. The door was open."

"The protection spells should have stopped you. Did you feel anything?"

"No." I wriggled desperately as the plant continued to coil around me.

She shook her head and sipped her drink before moving to her desk and shuffling some papers. "Humans. So utterly ignorant of magic, they can walk through wards without noticing."

"The, er, plant."

Pytha looked up and, at a wave of her hand, the plant unwound itself and snaked back into the jungle that covered her walls. "So, who are you and what do you want?"

"Noelle Bruma, I'm working in Fae Audits with Albert Ahrenns."

"Ah yes, the missing graduate." I winced. "Albert was quite worried about you. He called you several times."

I got out my phone and gulped. There were three missed calls from Albert and another two from Precious that I hadn't received in the murky bowels of London's underground train system. My stomach lurched. What did he think of me? That I was irresponsible and late, or maybe, my chest lifted with sudden hope, maybe he thought I was sick and hadn't phoned in because I was in hospital. It was odd that the best option my mind could come up with was hospitalisation and, for a second, I was tempted to go with it, until the more rational part of my brain chimed in that I was already in the office and I'd easily get caught out in a lie. No, I had to get to the fae realm and quick.

"Can you conjure up a portal, please?"

Pytha's laugh was like a summer breeze flowing through the treetops. "My dear, it's not that simple. Portals require requisition form two six four underscore P to be completed at least a week in advance." She handed me a form and behind me, something slithered along the wall.

"Isn't there anything you can do? I'm meant to be in the fae realm with the team."

She stopped shuffling papers and looked at me. "I used a lot of magic on the first portal."

There was something in her voice that made me bite my lip. She was fae, I was pretty sure of that, so she couldn't lie, and she hadn't answered my question directly.

"So, you can open another portal today? I mean, you are physically able to."

Pytha inclined her head.

"And, if I filled out this form, could you choose to waive the wait time?"

She eyed me. "Perhaps. I have discretion over which portals to open when, but, why would I move you to the front of the queue?"

I thought for a second. "You like gifts, right? I could bring you a box of chocolates, two, anything you want."

"Anything I want." The wistful tone of her voice wrapped around my chest like one of her vines.

Too late, I realised my mistake. I was in the middle of a bargain with a fae. "I mean, it's fine. I'll just go back up to our offices and wait. There's still paperwork up there I can do and I'll email Albert and let him know where I am so he can come and get me." I backed away.

"But you don't know what I want, young Noelle, it's nothing really. Just a small thing from you and you can join your team in the fae realm. Think what Albert will say about your initiative and how glad he'll be to see you." Her eyes gleamed in the greenish dappled light that made its way through the chinks in her plants' leaves.

Everything in me screamed that this was a bad idea, but she was more senior than me, and we worked for the same company. We were colleagues, so she wouldn't screw me over too much if we were on the same team, right? And I wanted to impress Albert so much. I had to do something to prove I was competent, to get his approval and stay on the fast track to a career in management and then onto a directorship.

"What's the bargain?"

Pytha grinned, a wild, hungry grin that exposed her sharp white teeth. "For you, a young graduate, I'll simply take a favour."

"A favour?"

"In exchange for opening one portal to join your audit team."

I searched through her words. "To open one portal *now* to join the team."

This time, her smile held some warmth. "Of course. Do you accept the terms?"

"Wait. This favour…it isn't something that will hurt me, will it?"

"Ah, you want the standard no harm clause."

"What other standard clauses are there?"

She held up one hand and ticked them off. "No death, no selling your soul or body, no physical harm to yourself or your loved ones, and since Rumpelstiltskin, no taking your first-born child."

"Or any child."

"Fine. But this favour is becoming less and less valuable." She sighed like it was hardly worth her time to make the portal anymore.

"OK, I agree."

Pytha clapped her hands together and grinned at me. A

section of scroll appeared in her clawlike hands, which she handed over with a flourish. I read it carefully to make sure it reflected what I'd agreed to and then signed with the quill she gave me and handed it back. With a snap of her fingers, the small scroll disappeared, and she waved her hands in a complicated series of spirals that made the portal appear.

"Pleasure doing business with you."

I gave her a nervous smile and stepped through the portal.

Chapter 26

Attention to detail is a skill that is often overlooked, but it's how I made my fortune; paying attention to the small things that others ignore. And with intricate legal documents, of course.

Elizabeth Bathory – *The First Disrupter*

I ran down the path to the manor, my squeaky suitcase bumping my legs and drawing attention. I ignored the stares of the local fae and apologised as I almost bumped into a gargantuan snail pulling a massive cart filled to the brim with some sort of turquoise fruit balanced atop of boxes stamped with maple leaves. It passed more quickly than I would have expected a snail could move and left a slippery silver trail in its wake, which I tiptoed through, lifting my suitcase so the wheels avoided the muck.

Panting hard, I made it to the manor and hurried into our workroom. Albert and Edwyn looked up from a stack of paperwork.

"Ah, there you are."

"Finally decided to show up," Edwyn sneered, and my face, already hot from the exertion of running here, turned beetroot.

"How did you make it here?" Albert frowned.

"I asked Pytha to conjure a portal."

"And she listened to you? I'm impressed." Albert shot me a smile, and I couldn't help the stupid grin that spread my lips as Edwyn scowled.

"There's lots to do. Get stuck in," he ordered.

I wheeled my suitcase to my shared room, poured myself a drink of crystal-clear water and dug into the pile of scrolls Edwyn had pointed at.

The day went quickly and mostly in silence until Precious and Tristan strolled back in. The orc settled into a chair and dusted off her hands. "And that is that."

"You've completed the asset test?" Edwyn sounded surprised. I smiled. Score one for the graduates.

"Yep."

"Well, I want the write up as soon as possible."

Precious pulled a face, but kept silent.

"Of course," Tristan said, limping to a chair and slumping into it. He slipped off his polished shoes, now dusty and more brown than black, and rubbed his feet.

"Winnie, come on. They've worked hard all weekend and they're exhausted after tramping all over the island. They can write it up tomorrow." Albert was the voice of reason.

"Of course, I just thought that–"

"We're well ahead of schedule. So much so that I'm heading back tonight. I'll come collect you on Friday, and I want to hear that Edwyn's been fair to you," Albert said to all of us.

If looks could kill, Edwyn's glare would have burned through Albert's bald head with laser precision. Albert left us to it and strolled out of the room. Edwyn threw his pen down on the table and stalked off to his bedroom. Since Albert wasn't staying, he'd procured the large double room for himself.

"Well, I'm tired. I'm off for a soak and then bed," Tristan announced before shambling off to his room, holding his shoes in his hands.

"I think I'll turn in too," Precious said. "Come with me."

I shook my head. "I've got a couple of things I want to do first." I had to make up for being late. "Don't wait up."

She shrugged but left me to it.

I pulled out a copy of the island map and checked it to my database. I was going to be thorough. And, yes, just as I thought, another exchange with the missing stone as collateral. I double-checked my database. That made three current contracts, all backed by a single stone that no one could find. That couldn't be right, could it? I was so deep in my work that I didn't notice anyone come in until Edwyn stood in front of me. Topless.

"What are you doing?"

I kept my eyes low on my screen. "I thought—"

"You thought you'd say that I made you work late."

The accusation made me raise my head to meet his angry eyes. "No, I wanted—"

"I don't know what your problem is, but I am this close to getting the promotion to senior manager and you are not messing that up for me." He leaned forward, and the scent of orange soap washed over me, tickling my nose.

"I don't want—"

"Let's get one thing straight. I don't care about you. I don't care about what you want. You are a naïve graduate in your first placement who thinks that hard work and keeping your head down will lead to recognition. Well, not here. Here, you have to look out for yourself, so the only thing I care about is that you listen to me; the person in charge of this audit. Do you understand?"

I nodded and looked down.

"Get to bed. I expect you up early tomorrow." With that, he stormed back into his room, leaving me gaping after him. Only a few years older than me and he acted like an overbearing father, bossing me about, telling me when my bedtime should be. An old spark of rebellion bloomed in my chest before I squashed it. I had learned long ago not to stand out, not to do anything that rocked fae status quo. Keep your head down, work hard, stay in control. That was my mantra.

I switched off my laptop and turned off the light before going to my shared bedroom. Precious was already asleep and snoring on top of the covers of her single bed. I got into my cotton pyjamas and slipped between my sheets, staring at the round moon that glinted through the window. Numbers and fae stones rolled around in my mind, and it was a long time before I could fall asleep.

~

"You are determined to make this difficult, aren't you?" Edwyn scowled at me. It seemed to be his default expression when dealing with me since the incident.

"What do you mean?"

"First, you can't do a simple physical asset test. Second, you cause rifts between me and Albert, and now you're determined to see things that aren't there. This is a simple enough audit, Elle. You tick off the account entries with the paperwork. Simple."

I placed my laptop on the table and pointed to the screen.

"I don't want to hear it, Elle. You want to be an auditor, so, audit. Don't come up with wild conspiracy theories about stones that aren't there. Do I need to write this up in your assessment?"

His fingers hovered over his keyboard and a small smirk played over his lips.

"But, I–"

Skathi swept in, his long robe folding gracefully around his ankles. "You've been working so hard, I thought I'd bring you in some tea." He took in the frosty atmosphere. "Is there a problem?"

"No." Edwyn glared at me.

I swallowed. I could say something and maybe there was a reasonable explanation for the discrepancy I'd found, but Edwyn had made it clear that my assessment was on the line. I needed to get a good score so they didn't throw me out of the programme and, even if they kept me on, I didn't want a black mark against my name. I could imagine what he'd write: troublemaker, difficulty following orders, not a team player. The words reverberated around my head, stealing away my chance of a career here.

"No," I echoed, taking my laptop back to my spot.

"Excellent. Now, Albert's told me this audit is on schedule and ready for Emperor Llyr's visit next week?"

"Absolutely," Edwyn said, "we're just tying up the final report."

"And do you have any questions for me? I know fae contracts can be a challenge if you're not used to them."

"We're good," Edwyn said, clipping out the two words.

"Excellent, well just call me if you need anything."

"Actually, I have a question," I said, risking Edwyn's ire.

"Excellent, a curious mind. Go on, go on," he replied,

settling himself in a chair.

"You use the fae stones instead of money."

"Yes, it's a very efficient system. No need to carry all your money around on your person."

"You can use banks for that." Precious leaned forward, taking some of Edwyn's anger off me.

"You trust someone else with your money?" Skathi's face screwed up in confusion. "Our system seems much simpler. No one can carry away one of the rocks."

"What about magic? A witch could levitate one away. Poof." Precious gestured with her hands to emphasise her point.

"These are fae stones. Magic cannot move them. Not even fae can move them. Safe as stones."

That made sense. If their currency was theft-proof, then maybe it was our financial system that was flawed.

"But, there are some exchanges here for jewels and gold and maple syrup," I persisted, pointing to a couple of the accounting entries.

"Ah, yes. Sometimes we are forced into material possessions, but I am a fae of simple means." He smiled and gestured around at his home. It was true, his furnishings were sparse, but they were exquisite, from the woven walls to the displayed statues. "Any more questions?"

"No." Edwyn's tone was final.

"Then I shall leave you to your auditing. I must say I envy

you, I have to leave as part of a delegation to the Winter Court to negotiate a treaty for the fae games; a process more tedious than watching paint dry. Ta-ra."

With that, Skathi left and Edwyn turned on us. "What the hell was that?"

"He said we could ask him questions."

"If there are questions about specific entries, those come through me in scheduled meetings that we minute, not off the cuff discussions about the fae banking system, and it's not our concern what he uses any money for."

"Unless it's for criminal activities or the proceeds of money laundering," I whispered. Some of those training videos really stuck in the mind.

"Very good. You've watched some compliance videos and read some textbooks. Welcome to the real world. I'm putting this in your assessments."

"But I didn't say anything," Tristan chimed in with a whine to his voice.

"For the love of– it's like babysitting." Edwyn turned on his heel and stalked off, still muttering to himself.

"Thanks for that." Tristan rounded on me and Precious. "I need this job."

"I should have stayed quiet." What was I thinking? Disobeying a manager, asking questions. My curiosity was going to get me in trouble. I needed to focus on learning the job and studying. Nothing more.

"We asked some questions, we didn't do anything wrong.

Albert will see that. Winnie's just being a little bitch because he's stressed about the promotion."

I smiled at Precious. I wished I had her composure. She oozed confidence, even when her jaw was tight and she was rattled. We all needed this job. We all wanted to stay. So, it was unfortunate when the next day, I found something that piqued my curiosity to new heights.

Chapter 27

Instincts – we all have them. I find it pays to follow them.

Elizabeth Bathory – *The First Disrupter*

"**P**recious, can you help me with something?" I asked.

"I'm in the middle of the August contracts," she replied, her gaze fixed on the spreadsheet on her screen.

"Please, it's urgent."

Edwyn looked up from his laptop. "Do you need her to wipe your arse for you?" He laughed at his own joke and Tristan brayed in unison. *Suck up.*

With a huff, Precious followed me to our bedroom, then stood, tapping her foot.

"Look," I said, pointing to three scrolls laid out on my bed.

"You took paperwork to bed with you. Girl, you need to get

laid."

"No, no. Look. Here." I pointed. "The same stones used as collateral for three different loans from the emperor."

"The emperor's lawyers–"

"Didn't spot it. Look at the smudges. I think someone deliberately did that so the stones couldn't be identified and, look." I shoved the map into her face. "It's the missing stone. It never existed. This is big, right? Fraud. Skathi's seal is on it, so it's fraud."

Precious screwed up her face. "You have to be sure about this. I don't like Edwyn. He's got it out for you."

I sank onto the bed. "I know. That's why I need your help."

She raised an eyebrow at me.

"I want to search the manor, see if there's something in his office to back this up. If anyone can get to his seal, maybe someone else used it on the document, or made a copy…" I trailed off. I sounded like a conspiracy theorist, but something in my gut told me that this was off and the numbers didn't lie.

"Sounds like it could be dangerous."

I sighed. "You're right. Sorry for asking. I'll…sort it out myself."

She grinned and cracked her neck. "I like danger."

"So, you'll help me?"

"Of course, us girls have got to stick together. And Skathi's left for the delegation, so tonight's the best time."

"Yes!" I held out my fist and she bumped it.

"Let's get back to work before they get suspicious."

I nodded, grabbed the papers and hurried back into the room. Two curious faces turned to us. Edwyn managed to have a sardonic edge to his look while Tristan's round eyes made him look like a puppy dog whose owner had hidden a stick behind their back.

"Well?" Edwyn asked.

"Uh," I mumbled.

"Period stuff," Precious came to my rescue.

I sat down as my face reddened. It seemed to confirm that something embarrassing had happened and the men turned back to their screens.

I tried to lose myself in the work for the rest of the day, but I was jumpy. Any time Edwyn asked me a question, I almost fell out of my chair and once I jumped so hard I spilled water all over a printed first draft of our audit report.

"What is going on with you today?" Was there an undercurrent of concern in Edwyn's voice? If there was, it was layered deep beneath his frustration.

"Nothing."

"We need to get this done. If you're sick, tell me and I'll draught someone else in to help."

"What? No! I'm fine." I didn't want to be kicked off the job. "Just…period stuff."

He shrank back, unsure how to cope with the menstrual cycle.

"I'm fine," I said again, and Edwyn left me alone with a curt nod, as if periods were something you could catch by being too close to the opposite sex.

"Glad I don't have to deal with that," Tristan said, listening in to our conversation.

"Men couldn't handle menstruation." Precious jutted out her jaw, daring him to disagree.

"Get on with your work," Edwyn interrupted, and we sank into silence.

At seven o'clock, Edwyn laid down his pen and shut his laptop with a click. "That's it for today. Ladies, clean up the leftovers, will you?"

Precious opened her mouth to say something about sexism, but I shook my head and she shut it with a grunt. This was perfect cover for us to sneak into the rest of the manor. Tristan left after him with a smirk on his plump lips.

As soon as they were gone, Precious started ranting sotto voce. "They think just because we've got vaginas, we should be the ones clearing up. I'd like to take one of these boxes and shove it where the sun doesn't shine."

"Shhh, they'll hear you." I gathered up the empty boxes into a pile and headed out of the office.

Precious followed me with her own pile of rubbish and we walked towards the kitchen. As soon as we left the workroom, one of the fae servants stopped us with a bow.

"May I assist you?"

"No," I paused. I had almost added a 'thank you' out of

habit, which the fae could take to mean that you owed them something. After my favour with Pytha and the portal, I wasn't getting entrapped again. "We're taking these to the bins."

"Allow me."

"We can do it," Precious scowled.

He backed up a step and then led the way to the kitchen. I stopped. "What's through that door?"

"That leads to Skathi's private rooms. The kitchen is this way."

"On second thoughts, why don't you take the boxes?" I faked a yawn. "We're pretty tired and it's an early start tomorrow."

He eyed me but took the pile with a half bow and headed to the kitchen.

"Come on," I said. I tried the door. "Locked." That was that then. We couldn't investigate. What a waste of time.

Precious bent to the lock and drew a dagger from somewhere under her clothes. She stuck the point into the lock and twisted, concentrating so hard, her pink tongue peeked out from behind her tusks. The door opened with a barely audible click.

Chapter 28

Preparation is everything. But, one should also be prepared for the unexpected. Did I expect to be turned into a vampire? No. But did it stop me from seizing the opportunity that a nearly immortal life offers? No. Adaptation combined with preparation makes one a formidable force in any area of life.

Elizabeth Bathory – *The First Disrupter*

W e scrambled inside and shut the door just in time to hear the servant's soft footsteps on the reed carpet in the hall. He mumbled something about leaving rubbish on the floor and there was a rustle as he removed the boxes Precious had dumped in the hall.

I held my breath until I was sure he had gone before gulping to wet my dry mouth. We were in a spacious corridor that had rooms coming off it at regular intervals on the left-hand side and one large door right at the end. Skathi's private rooms.

"Come on," I whispered.

Precious nodded and gestured for me to open the door. I swallowed, wishing my heart wasn't racing to get out of my chest, and turned the handle. Breaking the rules always led to trouble. The door swung inwards, revealing a green room with a huge painting of Skathi hanging on one wall. He wore a robe that left his torso uncovered. I couldn't believe our skinny host hid that many muscles under his clothes, but the strangest thing was that he was riding a giant painted snail, which reared up like a horse under him. It was like watching a car crash; you wanted to look away, but you couldn't.

"That painting is creepy on so many levels." Precious shivered.

I nodded and forced my eyes away from the painting to the rest of the room. There were two tables displaying ancient pottery, which was old enough to be worth a fortune, but not much else.

"If you look at it from the right angle, I don't think he's wearing anything under those robes…" Precious had moved closer to the picture, drawn like a moth to a flame.

I shook my head and, with a last glance at the painting, said, "Let's go."

She followed me to the next room. An enormous living desk dominated the space, green leaves sprouting from its squat legs. A bookshelf lined one wall, covered with scrolls and one token shelf filled with more traditional books. Large emerald green curtains hung against another wall. I pushed one back, revealing a large window that let in the shimmering lights of the dark fae sky, sending ripples of blue and purple into the room. A flash of red made me jump.

A shiver ran down my spine as the skies that had seemed magical when I first arrived now turned sinister, as if they didn't approve of what we were doing. I gulped as another streak of red wavy lights lit up the night. I did not want to end up in a horror film, but if Skathi had any incriminating paperwork, this was the place to find it.

I tried one of the drawers in the desk, half expecting it to be locked, so it was a pleasant surprise when it slid open without so much as a squeak. A smile lit up my face; we were in.

Precious riffled through a shelf of scrolls. "What are we looking for?"

"I don't know…something on the stones, any contracts that look dodgy."

She wrinkled her nose. "They all smell dodgy. What is that? Tea?"

"Maybe," I shrugged, "the fae do like their tea." I went back to the desk. Skathi had a paper diary, but there was nothing incriminating in it, just normal meetings. I flicked back a few pages and noticed one with Albert before the audit; it looked like they kept in touch outside of audit times. Managing audit clients must be one of a director's responsibilities, I shook my head; I had a lot to learn.

I opened another drawer and found a sharp letter opener and a gold fountain pen. "Look at this." I showed it to Precious.

She glanced over and turned back to the shelves. "So?"

"So, it's metal…"

"It's only iron the fae don't like. Or maybe silver, either way, gold is flashy but fine." She grinned and flipped her braids back to show me her gold hoop earrings and make her point.

The other drawers contained blank paper and I found an ancient mobile phone hidden in another. Dull.

"Did you find anything?" I asked, hoping that my colleague had come up trumps.

"I don't know. There's so many scrolls here and it's all in that stupid calligraphy. I wish I knew what to look for…wait, what was that?"

I froze.

"Someone's coming," Precious hissed.

I swore and shut the desk drawer. "The curtains." They were long enough to hide us, as long as no one looked closely at the two lumps in the emerald fabric.

I darted behind one and the rich material engulfed me, heavy and hot against my skin. Sweat beaded on my brow and I tapped my watch anxiously, but the familiar repetitive motion didn't calm me as I peeked out and whispered, "Hurry up."

Precious shoved the scrolls back on the shelf, swearing as they rolled onto the floor again. Her foot caught on one and she flung out an arm to the bookcase to catch herself, but her hand caught a book instead of the shelf. I watched with horror as it hinged down. Precious winced. And then stopped, the book not falling from the shelf and instead holding her weight.

She dangled there while a small panel slid out from the

bookcase revealing a secret room. My eyes widened and we locked gazes before a swish outside the door had me racing into the secret room. Precious grabbed the scrolls and raced inside, closing the panel behind her. We drew together in the confined space, our panting breath filling my ears. Heat poured off her and she swallowed, the sound harsh in the small room. My heart pounded so loudly, I was sure whoever was on the other side of the panel could hear. I clamped my lips together and clenched my fists as if that could stop our discovery.

Faint footsteps came closer. I tensed and Precious reached out and grabbed my hand. I squeezed back. Whatever happened next, we were in this together.

Chapter 29

Dear Abby, I don't have any special skills and the school talent show is in a week. My friends have signed me up, but I have no idea what to do. I'm only good at chemistry and I'm scared whatever I try, I'll mess it up. Help!

Honey, I get it, you're worried about making a fool of yourself (icing thought), or maybe you're worried that those bad thoughts in your head are real and you're worthless because you can't think of a special skill for the show (that's your first layer). But let me tell you; you are special, you don't need to take part in a talent show to prove that (bam – that's the gooey centre, honey and it is good!). Besides, you're good at chemistry, rig up something to explode, some of the science videos I've seen on the internet are pretty darn exciting. Go out with a bang. Fake it till you make it. And if something goes wrong, then improvise.

Yours cakefully, Abby.

Abby Wright – *Ask Abby*

We waited for an age, a decade, a century for the steps to walk around the room. Possible explanations fluttered through my head, but there was nothing that could adequately cover why we stood, hidden in a secret room with Precious clutching scrolls so tight that they had dents in the perfect spirals. A shadow crossed the paper-thin gap around the panel and I shrank closer to Precious.

This was bad. They would find us. We'd be kicked off the audit, they'd throw us in fae jail and, worse, we'd be fired. OK, maybe my priorities were in the wrong order. But it was bad, and I was so anxious that even my toes tapped as my body sought an outlet for my pent-up energy.

A world-weary sigh sounded on the other side of the panel, followed by the swish of heavy fabric moving as they drew the curtains closed and shut off even the dim light entering the room through the cracks around the panelling. More slow steps then the click of the door shutting.

"They're gone," Precious said, her voice barely more than a breath that tickled the top of my head.

"Wait," I said. And I counted to three hundred – five minutes – in my head while Precious became more and more fidgety.

I had got to two hundred and five when she huffed out a sigh. "Enough. There's no one there. We did it."

"Fine," I agreed, still counting in my mind. Now I'd started, I had to finish. I squinted and looked around the room. There were no windows, and it was pitch black.

"There must be a light."

I plucked my phone from my trouser suit pocket and found the torch. Cupping a hand around the light so it couldn't shine into Skathi's office, I directed it around the room. It was a smaller office. A wooden desk grew in here, too, but rather than leaves, it had curling silvery bark that lined its surfaces, giving it an eerie feel, as if it was only a ghost of the tree it could have been.

A statue in a thinking pose squatted in one corner, its pale marble skin shining under the meagre torchlight.

Smaller paintings hung on the walls. I thought I recognised a couple from museums, but if they were prints, they were good ones. Precious started on the desk and I studied the pictures. One of them was hung slightly askew. It shouldn't have mattered at a time like this, but I couldn't help myself. I reached out to straighten it and gasped as I discovered the safe.

I waved Precious over and took down the painting to reveal a solid wooden door with a small wheel embedded into it, similar to the safes you see in the movies, but more delicate and intricate with light and dark polished inlays that had been smoothed so it looked like a continuous surface. The scent of lemon and wax filled the air from the polish.

I grinned at Precious. Jackpot. If Skathi was doing anything dodgy, he'd keep any evidence in the safe. But how to open it?

Precious had her knife back out, and she slipped it round the edges. Nothing budged. She punched the safe in frustration. Her fist didn't leave so much as a mark in the thick wood.

"Sonofa– that hurt." She shook her fist out, then sucked her bruised knuckles. Brute force wasn't going to work on this door then.

"Maybe he wrote the combination somewhere." I turned to the desk and rifled through the drawers for a series of numbers. Nothing. No handy note with a significant birthday on it or a reminder not to forget the combination with an easy to break code.

I considered the wheel. It didn't look like there were numbers anywhere on it, which was weird, because safes had combinations, right? And didn't the wheels normally stick out? That's what they did in the movies. I reached out and touched the centre of the embedded wheel.

It raised out from the door with a smooth mechanical motion, so now I could turn it.

"Let's give it a spin." Precious reached for the wheel, but I put a hand on hers.

There was something about the safe that called to me…

The wood was patterned with intricate square and triangle inlays and the wheel looked like it ought to match up. I considered it and gently spun the wheel until one of the triangles matched up with part of the door. Nothing happened. I twisted again, and this time, the piece I fiddled with twisted on its axis. So, it had an x and a y axis. I moved it along in a rotation until a small section of the wheel matched with the pattern. Nothing.

I tapped the wheel with my fingernail as I thought and a piece of the wheel disconnected and slotted itself into the surface of the door, fitting in perfectly with the pattern.

"Woah," Precious said, leaning over my shoulder.

"Yeah, so maybe…" I twisted the wheel again, and noticed the patterning on the other side. This was like a puzzle or a Rubik's cube. A smile crept over my face. I'd always been good at Rubik's cubes. With a flick of my fingers, I sent one piece of the wheel spinning on its axis, then twisted the wheel, going through familiar motions as I solved the puzzle, one piece at a time.

Precious watched me with keen eyes. "That is some savant stuff right there."

I grunted and ignored her. I wasn't a savant, but I was going to solve this puzzle. "Hold my phone and keep the light steady." Two hands meant I could go twice as fast. That was the theory, anyway.

"There, that piece goes there."

I turned my head and looked at where she pointed. This would be a whole lot easier if we had a proper light in here. I pursed my lips as I thought along three axes and then made the moves to slot the piece into its place. Soon, I entered the calm zone that my brain always found when tackling logic puzzles like this. Nothing more than an extra complicated Rubik's cube. I could see the algorithms as I worked them through, twisting and turning each segment. Twenty-seven pieces later and we were done.

The safe door swung open an inch. I wiped the sheen of sweat from my brow and held out my fist to Precious, who bumped it with a grin.

"Girl, that was amazing."

I grinned back. Yeah, I was pretty amazing when it came to logic and maths. "Just a simple algorithm. You should see what I can do on a pool table."

She gave me look that was part disbelief, part awe.

I smiled as pride swelled through me. "Well, maybe not so simple…let's see what Skathi has hidden in here."

I opened the door all the way and reached inside, my fingers feeling like they brushed invisible cobwebs as I stretched in and grabbed the papers. I took my phone back and scanned the documents. Unlike the scrolls, these were printed on ordinary paper and they showed notarised copies of Skathi's signature using the same stone for multiple loans. We had him. I snapped some photos.

"Wait, there's something in the back." Precious shoved her arm into the safe and pulled out a small velvet bag, which she emptied on the silver birch desk. Diamonds. And was that a bottle of maple syrup? I checked the label, it read PREMIUM SYRUP.

I looked around. Something felt off. When the orc's arm had reached into the safe, that same web sensation I got from walking through Pytha's portals had brushed over me and now it rushed over me like strands of thread before focusing at the far end of the room.

I stared at the wall while Precious studied the diamonds. Had there always been a statue half in / half out of the wall?

"Precious?"

"Hang on, I'm getting a picture." She held up a large stone to her ear and took a selfie. A smoky smell curled into my nostrils.

"Precious."

"I said, hang on." She shook my hand off her arm.

"We need to go."

"In a minute."

"We need to go. Now." I shoved her. She looked up, irritated at my interruption, before following my gaze to where a colossal statue now filled one half of the secret room, having prised itself from the wall. It lurched towards us.

"A guardian! Schiztz," she swore. "Should have known he'd have something guarding the safe. Run!"

I ripped my gaze from the gigantic tree man as he wrenched himself from the wall and took a step towards us with a sound that was a cross between ripping wood and a hurricane.

Chapter 30

When you're backed into a corner, all you can do is fight or roll over. And I'm not one to roll over.

Elizabeth Bathory – *The First Disrupter*

We ran across the small room to the panel that led to the study. Precious scrabbled for the switch to get us out while I gave unhelpful updates that the creature was getting closer.

The guardian's eyes glowed a fearsome reddish orange behind its twisted wooden face. It lurched towards us, crunching through the silvery desk like it was a pile of sticks. The smoky smell of burning wood combined with something sweet, like roasting apples, filled the room.

It fixated on us, coming closer. I held up the stack of paper I'd grabbed like a weapon. The monster brushed aside my papers, sending them fluttering to the ground.

"There's been a mistake," I tried, then I ducked as it swung its clawed branch of an arm at me. So it wasn't one for talking.

Precious shoved herself in front of me, her knife back in her hand. She crouched low and sprung up at the creature, plunging her blade into its wooden skin with a war cry that had me cringing back. It shook her off, like getting stabbed was no more annoying than a mosquito bite.

"Find a way out!" Precious said between gritted teeth as she yanked her weapon free and struck again.

I tore my gaze away from the fight and worked my fingers around the panel, searching for the mechanism that would free us. Precious bumped against me, flattening me to the wall as she avoided the guardian's blow.

She dived again. I shone my phone's torch around and found a small switch. I flicked it. The panel slid open with a neat click. I grabbed Precious and pulled her through.

We leaned against the panel, desperate to shut the guardian in its room.

"Maybe it will go back to being part of the wall now we've left," I said, voicing the desperate hope that bubbled in my chest.

The panel shook under the weight of the guardian's blow. The small amount of hope I had snuffed out. I swallowed, pushing against the panel with all my strength. This was how I would die. Because I was too curious. Because I disobeyed orders from my manager. Bad things always happened when you didn't follow the rules.

"We should call for help," I whispered.

"Fat lot of good that would do. We're the ones who broke in. No one's going to help us."

My mind raced as the next thud rebounded through my body, clacking my jaw together. "Do you think you can take it from behind?"

Precious nodded, her face grim, but she made a joke anyway. "That's what he said."

There must have been something in the air, or maybe it was the adrenaline that jittered through my veins, because I snorted out a laugh at her gallows humour. We were about to die, why not laugh? Tristan had obviously rubbed off on us. The double entendre made me giggle again.

"OK, so we're going to let it in." Precious looked at me as if I was mad. Maybe I was. But this had to work. "Trust me."

"With my life." She reached out and grasped my forearm in a warrior's grip. I squeezed her forearm back. We were sisters in arms.

"On three. One…Two…Three." We sprang away from the panel and pressed ourselves flat against the unmoving shelves.

The guardian rammed the door again and, with no resistance, fell through into the room. Precious leapt, clenching her dagger tight in her fist. She landed on its back and stabbed it again and again in its thick head. The sickening crunch of metal into wood and splitting bark filled the room. Why hadn't anyone heard and come to investigate? I edged towards the door. I had to get help.

The creature roared – a sound like a tree hit by lightning – and flailed, reaching behind its back with its rough wooden arms, clawing at Precious. She ignored the cuts it opened in her green flesh and squared her jaw as she plunged the dagger into its skull.

With another roar, the guardian crushed Precious against a wall. Her blade slipped from her hand and landed on the floor with a dull clunk. She wrapped her muscular arms around its neck in a choke hold and squeezed the hard wood. It dived forward and she catapulted over its head and into a wall. There was a loud crack. She slumped to the floor.

"Precious!" I couldn't help the shout that erupted from my mouth. The monster turned and focused its fiery eyes on me.

I swallowed and ran for the door, all pretence of sneaking gone as I fled for my life. The creature moved to block me, its long legs easily eating up the distance in the study. I backed up, facing it and held out my phone, the torch still on.

It winced and blinked at the sudden sharp light aimed at its face. I ducked to the side and groped for the door handle, still aiming for flight over fight. It recovered and swiped at me, its clawed hands connecting with my stomach and sending me flying into the bookshelf.

I whimpered and fell to the ground, doubled over in pain. It loomed over me, a dark shadowy figure from a nightmare. I closed my eyes and held up my hands to protect my face. Its rough hands gripped mine. I braced in expectation of the oncoming pain.

But there was nothing. I opened my eyes and stared up into the still form of the guardian, frozen. No fire burned behind its eye holes. I wrenched my hands free of its grip and scuttled away across the floor. It didn't follow. Keeping my gaze on the frozen guardian, I made my way to Precious and checked for a pulse.

There was a heart-stopping moment where I couldn't find one, until I shifted my grip from her wrist to her neck and found a slow, steady heartbeat pumping under her skin. She was alive. I shook her, then slapped her face.

Her green eyes blinked up at me, out of focus for a second before she pushed herself up, fists up, ready for a fight. She stared at the guardian, then at me. "Woah. You stopped it."

"Yeah, and I don't know how, so we need to go."

She patted herself down. "That's a waste of a good dress…" Her hand went to her waist and panic flickered over her face. "My dirk. The knife."

"Let's go."

"Not without my dirk." She scanned the floor and retrieved the blade from the woven carpet, wiping something brown and sludgy on the plush curtains before sheathing the dagger back under her clothes. I eyed the statuesque guardian, my heart beating so fast I was sure it would give up any minute. "Now we can go…" Precious trailed off, eyeing the doorway.

I turned. A dark figure stood silhouetted in the door. It stepped forward and fae lights flared around the room. Skathi was home.

Chapter 31

If you're offered a choice between life or death, I think that most of us would choose to live, no matter the consequences. I know I did.

Elizabeth Bathory – *The First Disrupter*

Skathi took it all in. Our dishevelled appearance. The splintered remains of the panel that hid his secret room now littering his carpet. The still guardian. His mouth fell open before he recovered and narrowed his dark eyes at us.

"Ladies, what are you doing in my private rooms?"

"Er…looking for paperwork." My stupid brain failed to come up with a lie. Precious gave me a look that told me I was an idiot, but she clamped her mouth shut and crossed her arms over her chest.

"I see. Take a seat. And before you decide to do something stupid, orc, if you so much as take one step towards me or the door, I'll have you tied up in vines quicker than you can say 'For the clan'. Now, sit."

We both sank onto the carpet. Skathi nodded and headed to his secret room.

"What's going to happen to us?" My mind raced with a hundred different possibilities, none of them good.

Precious shrugged, her gaze darting to the door, the secret room and the window, eyeing an escape. Skathi reappeared.

"Who helped you?"

I blinked. That was not the question I was expecting. "What?"

"Only a fae mind could open that safe, so who on my staff helped you? Answer now, and I might spare you."

"If anything happens to us, the Bathory Corporation will know about it," Precious said, still defiant from her position on the floor.

Skathi's smile was cruel, like a fox who knows he has the chickens cornered and is now just biding his time, playing with them, before he strikes the killing blow. "A tragic accident. Two foolish, young employees go on a night walk in the fae realm, heedless of the warnings of monsters that roam the land. Regrettable." He sighed. "There will probably be a nice ceremony, a memorial, a payout to your families. But accidents do happen. Of course, the price of audits might go up, and the emperor will probably decide to change audit company to distance himself from any scandal, but you won't care about losing your company money. You'll be dead."

"You can't lie," I said. "They'll never believe that story."

His smile grew more pointed, like a blade. "Fae can't lie, but you would be amazed at how well we can stretch the truth; a slight nuance can give us all the loopholes we need. Now, tell me who helped you."

"No one helped us," Precious answered. "Moron."

"I don't like your tone." With a flick of his wrist, creeping vines surrounded Precious. She squirmed, trying to fight them off, but they tangled around her, pinning her arms to her body and then wrapping around her neck and mouth. "Now, why don't you tell me everything and I might decide to give you a memory potion instead of killing you? Bodies are just so messy. I don't want to kill you. But I will, if I have to."

I swallowed, willing some moisture back into my dry mouth. I believed him. Skathi was fae and couldn't lie. "No one helped us," I croaked.

"You expect me to believe that a human and an orc opened an enchanted fae safe by themselves and then deactivated the guardian of this room…you want death, don't you?"

"No! OK, I'll tell you what happened…" I thought quickly. He wanted someone to be guilty. I hated lying, but our lives depended on it and I wasn't fae, not bound by their wordplay and loopholes. "But first, I want your oath that you won't hurt us."

"You have no bargaining power here."

"Then you'll never know how we got in." I held my breath.

"Fine, I swear on everyone I hold dear that I won't harm a

single hair on your heads."

I swallowed again. "OK, someone let us in, said something about some papers we had to see for the audit. I don't know their name."

"You're lying. Have it your way."

"You swore you wouldn't harm us."

"I swore I wouldn't harm a hair on your pretty little head, I didn't say anything about your skin. Now, let's go. I don't want to get blood on my carpet."

He yanked me to my feet and I cursed my stupidity. Never make a bargain with a fae.

A rush of magic sucked through the room, brushing over my skin like a piece of lace; scratchy yet soft at the same time.

"Who did you call?" Skathi's eyes narrowed.

"No one," I whispered.

"Then why is a portal opening?"

Chapter 32

Anyone who tells you that luck doesn't play a part in life is a liar. But that doesn't mean you can't make your own luck.

Elizabeth Bathory – *The First Disrupter*

"Wait here and don't do anything stupid," Skathi ordered. He stood, smoothed down his robes and left. I heard him mutter something over the shut door and a hum of magic buzzed against my senses.

Certain he was gone, I scooched over to Precious and pulled at the vines. They didn't budge. She motioned with her eyes to her lower half and mumbled a word behind her gag. It took me a couple of seconds to understand that she wanted me to get her knife.

I guessed where her waist was under the mass of vines that no longer writhed over her body but instead gripped her tight like leafy, green rope. I worked my fingers between two strands, easing my hand under the ropes until I felt the fabric of her dress. My eyes went to her face, and she gave me more signals; down and to the left. I moved round until I felt something lumpy and metallic. The dagger. I gripped it between two fingers and eased it out, sweat dripping down my brow. If I slipped, I could cut her, or myself.

Sometimes, I wish my mind wouldn't always go to the worst outcome. It was as if it was a separate person that couldn't ever believe that I might succeed. I forced myself to ignore it and the wave of compulsion that was sure to come and focused on wriggling the dagger free. It snagged on the vines. The gap I'd slipped my fingers through wasn't big enough.

I glanced at Precious. She rolled her eyes at me before making a side-to-side motion with her head. Of course. *Idiot.* I could saw through the vines. Angling the blade away from her body as much as I could, I gently sawed at the trailing plant. It took an age, but as the dagger cut through, I had more movement and a better angle. The knife cut through with a singing noise and I gave a whoop of triumph before setting down the blade and unwrapping the vines like she was some sort of plant mummy.

The stem was thick and had moulded itself to fit Precious, but with some effort, I unwrapped her torso. As soon as her arms were free, Precious yanked the plant off her face and then tore at the remaining vines around her legs.

"Are you OK?"

"Been better." She shot me a grin. "Been worse, too. Let's go."

"He spelled the door. We're stuck. Unless you want to break a window."

Her grin broadened, and she picked up the chair behind the desk as if it was nothing. With a grunt, she chucked it at the thin glass. The window shattered and cool night air poured in.

Precious vaulted out with an athleticism I could never match. In her torn dress and covered with cuts, she looked like an ancient warrior, the type that you get in fantasy games where the female armour barely covers their breasts or butts, but I had to admit, she could pull it off.

I followed more cautiously, positioning the chair so I could climb up to the sill. Then I stopped. The papers. I dashed to the secret room and grabbed as many as I could while Precious hissed at me to hurry up. This was evidence that would show Skathi's guilt. Gripping them tight against my chest, I stepped onto the chair, wobbled onto the windowsill and jumped down. I landed more heavily that the orc, despite our size difference, and winced at the impact to my ankles.

I beamed up at her. Despite our wounds and the horror of fighting for our lives against a magical guardian and being captured, it finally felt like something was going right.

We crept round the house, sticking to the shadows, not knowing if Skathi had set guards or who we could trust. The sky flashed with ethereal colours, lengthening every shadow and making each mundane shape seem sinister. My heart jumped out of my chest with every flicker of light that revealed nothing more menacing than a tree or house, made unnatural by the dark. I clutched the papers to my chest as if they were a shield for my fears, and maybe it worked, because the only compulsion that raced through me was that something terrible would happen if I dropped them. So, I crushed them to me as we moved around the manor.

At the front, Precious slowed and peered round the corner like she was a leading commando in a war movie. "Skathi's coming back and there's someone with him," she said, ducking back to my side.

"Schiztz," I swore in Dwarfish. I'd been through enough foster homes and schools to have heard every kind of language and let me tell you, nothing beats Dwarfish when you need to cuss. "OK, we wait for him to go inside then sneak back to our rooms, hide the evidence and tomorrow we fake an illness and get back to the safety of headquarters."

"Good plan. Only one problem." She jerked a thumb back round the corner. "Edwyn just came out. I could hear him."

I swore again. "What's he talking to Skathi about?"

She tilted her head, trying to pick out the words. "Not sure. We're too far away but look." I followed her finger with my eyes. Lights pricked on around the mansion.

"That's not good." I squeezed the paperwork tighter.

"Oh no, Albert's here too."

"What?" I peeked round the corner and saw his round form silhouetted by the fae lights that had appeared in the garden. "He's not meant to be here until Friday…We need to get back to our rooms before anyone figures out where we've been."

"I think it's too late for that." I peered up at Precious, taking in the pained look on her face. "I heard someone say 'missing'. They're looking for us."

"OK, OK, so we say we were out for a nighttime stroll, sorry for causing so much trouble, but we're here now, ha, ha. Everyone goes home happy."

"That's your plan." Precious gave me a stare of disbelief. "Look at us." She gestured to her ragged dress and my bruises.

"OK, so we were out for a stroll, and we were attacked." I was aware of the irony of using Skathi's threat as an alibi, but I couldn't come up with an original idea.

"And the papers?"

I shoved them under my shirt. Precious raised an eyebrow. Yeah, my thin cotton shirt didn't do much to hide anything.

"Then we come clean. Tell them everything."

Precious huffed out a breath.

"I'm sorry, do you have a better idea?" The stress brought out my sarcasm.

"No." She pinched her nose. "OK, but we have to avoid Skathi."

"Obviously. Is he still there?"

Precious peered round the corner again. "No."

"OK, let's go."

"Go where, ladies?" A familiar voice sounded behind our backs. Skathi had found us.

Chapter 33

Every action has a consequence.

Elizabeth Bathory – *The First Disrupter*

My heart threatened to jump out of my mouth before it sank all the way to my sensible shoes. I turned to see Skathi, looking a little more dishevelled than usual and pointing a pink crystal at us like it was a gun.

"I suppose you thought that you could escape."

We kept quiet, pressing back against the wall of the manor.

"I don't know how you called the emperor here, but this complicates things. I will have to dispose of you now and worry about the alibis later."

"The emperor is here?" The words were out of my mouth before I could stop them. I didn't know how he'd got here but he had, and we had the paperwork to implicate Skathi in a fraud. We had to get to him. Precious looked at me and nodded. She'd come to the same realisation.

With a war cry that sounded across the island, she launched herself at the fae. A pink spark flew from the crystal, hitting her shoulder, and then she was on him. The stench of burning flesh stung my nostrils. Her powerful form drove him to the ground with a thud, and they rolled.

"Run!" she yelled as I stood there wondering how I could help.

I couldn't. That was the truth. I was a wispy girl with no muscles and no combat experience, but I could darn well get the papers to the right person. I fled over the manicured lawn to the front door and ran into Albert.

"Elle? Thank goodness." He placed his meaty hands on my shoulders and looked me in the eyes. "Are you alright? Where's Precious?"

"She's fighting with Skathi."

"Good god. What's got into her?"

"No, you don't understand. He's committing fraud. I've got the evidence here." I pulled the paperwork out from under my shirt and pressed it into his hands. "It's all here."

The adrenaline waned. I felt heavy and tired. I shook my head.

"This is a very serious accusation…" he eyed me, "…but, perhaps we should talk about it after we've rescued Precious." He thought for a moment and muttered under his breath, "Or Skathi."

I had no time to wonder how he planned to rescue my friend,

because a tall, older fae with a patrician nose and greying hair swept out of the house.

Albert bowed. "Emperor Llyr."

My eyes widened, and I did a strange motion somewhere between a bow and a curtsey. It was not elegant.

"Please, Precious. She's in trouble." I pointed to where I had last seen them.

"Come." The emperor's voice was deep and commanding. Albert and I fell into step behind him as he strode over the lawn. The sounds of the scuffle – grunts combined with meaty hits and the occasional cry – grew louder as we approached.

"Enough." With a wave of his hand, the emperor bound Precious and her assailant with magic and parted them. "What is the meaning of this?"

"She hit me, your majesty." Blood poured from Skathi's nose and his speech was thick, as if he struggled to breathe.

"Only because he attacked us!" Precious now sported a bloody lip and her clothes were singed as well as torn. Skathi looked worse.

"Come. I will get to the bottom of this." The emperor led the way to the manor, levitating Precious and Skathi behind him as he strode through the door to a suite of guest rooms.

"I'll let everyone know to call off the search, I know that the team has been worried," Albert excused himself, rifling through the papers as he went.

"We will wait." Once he had sat down on a plush chair and accepted tea from the servants, the emperor eyed us all. "Sit," he commanded.

I perched on the edge of a floral chaise longue, worried about getting the pale fabric dirty. Precious and Skathi were forced onto a sofa, still bound by whatever magic the fae emperor wielded. We waited in silence until Albert returned, still holding the papers. Some of the tension eased from my shoulders. We still had the evidence.

"Now, what happened?"

"They broke into my office and then she attacked me," Skathi started.

"Is this true?" Albert's face was a mask of horror. "You breached a client's privacy?"

I hung my head. "We were looking for evidence."

"I am surprised and disappointed that you took such a reckless risk, and went against company policy no less. Please, forgive them, your majesty. I can assure you we take any breach of privacy very seriously."

The emperor waved away Albert's words and focused his attention on me. "What crime were you looking for evidence for?"

I swallowed. "Fraud. He's used the same fae stone as collateral for multiple loans."

Llyr raised one perfect eyebrow. "Indeed. And did you find any evidence?"

"Yes, in the safe."

"I know Skathi has many enchantments to protect his

security, so tell me, how did you manage to break into a fae-charmed safe?"

"I solved the puzzle."

He raised his other eyebrow at my mumbled answer. "And Skathi, a charmed safe was your only defence? You almost deserved to be robbed." Was that a hint of amusement in the emperor's voice?

"There was a guardian spell, too," Skathi said with a hint of defiance.

"And that failed?"

Precious snorted. "No, that activated. What do you think ruined my dress?"

"Really? And how did you defeat it?"

She shrugged. "I was unconscious."

I shifted as the emperor's full attention turned to me. "*You* defeated the guardian?"

"No, I don't think so. It just ran out of juice." I saw the disbelief on their faces, so I expanded. "It had me cornered, but then it just sort of died. But the important thing is that we have the evidence. Albert has it."

He nodded and handed the papers to the emperor. "They're telling the truth. And, from my team's physical asset test, the fae stone referenced in these multiple loans doesn't even exist."

Emperor Llyr read the papers in detail, pausing to reread pages as he flicked through. The fae's attention to detail was incredible, must be because they spent so much time twisting their words to get the best out of every situation and making sure they weren't stuck in contracts they had no intention of keeping. Skathi's wordplay still rankled me.

Eventually, the emperor looked up from the papers. "I see. It would seem that Skathi has used the fabricated stone to collateralise loans to purchase maple syrup. No doubt to cause price rises or possibly to seek to show that I cannot maintain a stable currency."

"Your majesty–"

"Save your breath, Skathi. Did you think I wouldn't notice how you've hoarded syrup? That's why I'm here. And how fortuitous that I arrived in time to prevent harm. As for the Bathory Corporation…"

Albert stiffened. I gripped Precious' hand.

The emperor smiled at us. "I am indebted to your two intrepid team members, Precious Sturmrock and Noelle Bruma." My head snapped up, he had just put himself in debt to us. Fae never did that. He met my gaze. "And I do not say that lightly." He turned to Albert and steepled his fingers. "I do not wish for these ladies to be disciplined for revealing this fraud to me."

"No, of course not." Albert gave us a fatherly smile. "They were just doing their jobs. A bit enthusiastically, perhaps, but the important thing is that we've uncovered this fraud so we can stop it."

"Indeed. Lord Skathi will be punished according to our

laws."

The fae blanched. "Imperial Majesty, please, I…"

The emperor held up his hand. "You may make your pleas to the Court. Take him away."

His guards must have supernatural hearing because Llyr didn't raise his voice to summon them, but they entered the room the instant he spoke and dragged Skathi out, still protesting.

"So, you can release me from your spell," Precious said once Skathi was gone.

"Naturally. My apologies." He nodded and the invisible bindings were gone, leaving Precious to stretch and sit more comfortably on the sofa.

"Now, I request a word with Noelle."

Albert and Precious both lifted their eyebrows at me, and my spine stiffened. A private meeting with the fae emperor couldn't be a good thing. The adrenaline that had just left my body raced back through my veins.

"I'll wait for you outside," Precious said, placing a large hand on my shoulder and giving me a squeeze before she left. She was a good friend, and our illicit night-time activities had bonded us in a way no audit could.

Once they left, the room seemed much larger and more intimidating. I clenched my fists in the sofa's fabric. It was time to face the emperor.

Chapter 34

No one is what they seem. Everyone has a hidden side to themselves.

Elizabeth Bathory – *The First Disrupter*

mperor Llyr regarded me for a long moment, his glittering black eyes pulling my gaze to his. I shifted under such intense attention.

"Noelle…"

"Elle. Call me Elle."

He smiled, "Elle, I struggle to understand how a young human could break into an enchanted fae safe and defeat a guardian."

My mouth opened and closed like a goldfish before I found some words. *"I told you, I solved the puzzle on the safe. It* wasn't magic, it was maths."

"Are you fae?"

"No." There was an edge of bitterness to my voice. I was human. No magic powers. I'd wished for them throughout my life, especially at my lowest points, but they'd never materialised. I was just an unwanted human with no family.

"Then why did the puzzle reveal itself to you?"

"No idea. I don't know anything more than I've said." I tilted my chin up in defiance. I was exhausted and in pain and this questioning was pointless. "Maybe the safe was broken."

He raised an eyebrow and his lips twitched as if I'd said something funny. "Broken…Skathi is a cautious fae with strong magic. He would not take a chance with his secrets, no fae would. No, Elle," his voice deepened as he said my name and the intensity of his gaze ratcheted up to an inferno that made my stomach squirm. He stood and walked over to me, cupping my chin with his soft hand. "There is more to you than meets the eye."

I swallowed, captured by his gaze. No one had ever paid me this much attention. It compressed my chest and my blood rushed to my face. I licked my lips and shifted on the sofa, unsure how to respond.

"I shall watch your career with interest, Elle." His voice made my name seem like an intimate secret that the two of us shared. I broke away. It was too much. He was too powerful and he must have done some magic to fog my thoughts, because all logic had left my mind and I couldn't think. He stepped back, giving me space. I took it as a dismissal, stood and hurried from the room.

Outside, I could breathe again.

"Tell me what happened," Precious said, pushing herself up from the wall she had been leaning against.

"Nothing. He just…didn't believe me about the safe." I couldn't put into words the subtext of the strange audience with the emperor. I wasn't even sure I knew what it meant myself, let alone to explain it to someone else. Did he think I was a supernatural? He hadn't said as much, but had he implied it? My head hurt from the fae's word trickery. I was certain of only one thing; I was now on the fae emperor's radar, and that seemed like a dangerous place to be.

"You look pale."

"I'm just tired."

"Breaking and entering will do that to you," she snorted.

"Why do I get the impression you're speaking from experience?"

She shrugged and gave me a saucy grin. "Let's get some sleep." So, she wasn't going to answer my question. What had Precious done before she got onto the graduate scheme? She brushed away my questions all the way back to our set of rooms, where Albert, Edwyn, and Tristan waited.

Tristan stopped his pacing as we entered. His mouth fell as he took in Precious' nearly naked body covered in scrapes and cuts. He hurried over and gave her his jacket, draping it over her shoulders.

Precious stared down at him. "You think my body is something to be ashamed of?" She shrugged off his jacket and left him gaping after her as she strode to our bedroom.

"No, I didn't–," Tristan stammered as he followed her, "I just thought –"

She slammed the door in his face and left him staring at the woven door before he stomped into his own room.

Albert looked at me, his face full of concern. "Are you alright? How did it go?"

"It was fine." I hugged my arms around myself.

"You didn't make him any promises, did you?"

I thought back over my conversation with the emperor and shook my head.

"Good," he sagged with relief, then rubbed his hands. "Well, congratulations on a great audit, team. We'll pack up tomorrow and submit the report. I think it's safe to say that we can't sign off on these accounts." Some tension seeped back into his body. "I'll let the executives know tomorrow. For now, I need some sleep." With that, he bustled back into his room. I could almost see him rehearsing his speech on the way. It was good to know I wasn't the only one nervous of the Bathory Corporation.

Edwyn stood and looked at me, his arms folded over his chest. "You're alright, then."

I nodded.

He opened his mouth and his expression softened as if he had more he wanted to say to me, but then his jaw tightened and he ground out, "Glad you're back, Bruma."

"I didn't know you cared, Winne," I replied using his hated pet name. I needed to stand up for myself more and letting my senior manager know that I wasn't a meek robot who followed his orders without thinking was as good a place as any. It's not like he could have a worse opinion of me.

He glared at me and marched to his room, now back to sharing with Tristan. I watched him go with a smile on my face, not knowing why it felt so good to get the last word in and needle the manager, but it did. It was like I'd grown up, realised my worth.

Abby would probably have a fancy name for it, but it felt like I'd reclaimed a little of my power, power which I hadn't realised had trickled away through a hundred minor – and a couple of major – infractions since I'd started.

Still riding my new high of standing up for myself, I headed to my shared room where Precious' snores already reverberated through the walls.

Chapter 35

*You won't get anywhere without recognising opportunities
when they knock on your door. Seize every opportunity that
comes your way, grab it with both hands and clutch it tight.
Fight for it, earn it and say yes. Most importantly, say yes.*

Elizabeth Bathory – *The First Disrupter*

"**E**lle, can I have a word?"

Those words were never good. I swallowed and followed Albert into one of the small meeting rooms and sat down on the edge of a grey chair, plucking the edge of my new skirt suit and racking my brains. What had I done wrong now? The fae audit was closed. The time to fire me would have been after the Emperor had taken Skathi away, not now, a couple of weeks later. Unless they had to wait to make it look like it wasn't related to the audit. I swallowed again.

Albert grinned at me from across the table and leaned

forward, placing both elbows on the white tabletop and resting his jowly chin in his palms.

"It can be hard to get on, Elle, especially as a human here at Bathory Corporation. But, I like you and I think we have a good understanding of one another. I wanted to let you know that I'll vouch for you at the Selection."

"Really?" I whispered the word, not daring to believe it.

"It's just before the end-of-year bash. So, if you keep your head down, work hard and stay quiet, then I'll look out for you."

A tension I'd held in my chest since day one eased. I'd get through the Reaping. Albert would vouch for me. "Thank you."

He rubbed his hands together, pleased with my answer. "There's a space coming up in my team…is that something you'd be interested in?"

It took me a second to catch up with Albert's words. So, I wasn't being fired?

"Yes!" I sounded too keen. My chest swelled with pride. This promotion would fast track my career, but I didn't want to look desperate. "I mean, yes, I'd definitely consider that as one of my options."

"Good, good. Well, I look forward to working together in the future. Let's get you through the Reaping first." He winked and left me sitting there, puzzled but happy. This was my dream; to have someone acknowledge my hard work, to get a step closer to being the youngest director at the company. He'd practically offered me a promotion, less than three months in my first job, and I wasn't even qualified yet. This was better than my wildest dreams, and I'd had some crazy dreams about getting promoted.

Edwyn came into the office with Precious in time to see Albert leave. "What was that about?"

"Albert just wanted to talk to me about a promotion."

"Congratulations, girl." Precious gave me a fist bump and grinned, her bottom teeth protruding over her red lips.

Edwyn scoffed. "Yeah, right. Wait. You're serious? He's talking to you about the senior manager position in the department? I've been working for that role for two years. What did you do?" He curled his lip at me. "Did you sleep with him?"

"What? No!"

"He forced you!" Precious stood, full of anger and concern. "'Cos you know if anyone tries anything, you just knee them in the balls." She mimed the action with enough vigour that Edwyn winced and took a step away from the tall orc. "You should come to my self-defence class."

"He didn't force me."

"Then what? Because from what I can see, all you've done is make our audit harder than it should have been, caused problems for our client and the company and there's no way you could be a senior manager here. You haven't got what it takes, so what did you do?" Edwyn glared at me, as if it was my fault that Albert had talked to me.

"He didn't promise anything. He just mentioned it. And he didn't say senior manager…" From graduate to senior manager, skipping all the roles in between…if I got that position, I'd be even closer to my goal of becoming a director here. But maybe I'd misunderstood. And Edwyn still glared at me. I swallowed. "I'm sure there will be a fair interview process if it comes to anything."

"You have no idea how anything works here, do you? If a director talks to you about a role, invites you to apply for it, then it's as good as yours. It's not what you know, it's who you know and I don't know what you've done to butter him up, but I'm onto you, Bruma. I'm onto you." With that, he turned on the heels of his smart brogues and stormed out of the door.

"He has got a stick so far up his arse, I'm surprised he can walk," Precious said.

I frowned. "He's right though."

"Don't listen to him. He's sour as vinegar about you being better than him."

"No. Listen. I'm not qualified. I've been here less than a quarter. I've done one audit. And I have caused trouble." I listed the reasons I shouldn't get the job on my fingers. "So, why would Albert even consider me? There's something I'm missing."

"I wouldn't overthink it. You're good. And we're going out for drinks tonight."

Chapter 36

Networking is an important skill, one everybody should learn. Too often, it's who you know, not what you know, that gets you ahead.

Elizabeth Bathory – *The First Disrupter*

Precious tapped her way over to where I sat at the bar with a couple of the other more introverted graduates on our programme, her hips catching the beat of the music perfectly.

"I need a drink," she gasped, ignorant of what her dancing had done to the majority of men and some of the women in the club. A couple of people followed her to the bar and stood to one side, vying for her attention with offers of drinks, which she ignored. When one of them dared to touch her on the forearm, she twisted his arm so far up behind his back that his eyes pricked with tears.

"If I was interested, I'd let you buy me a drink, but I'm here with my friends, so drop it before I drop you. Now, you nod."

He nodded and she let go.

"Impressive," I said.

She lifted one shoulder in a half shrug. "Not really. If he could have got free, maybe he'd be worth my time."

"What you need, Presh, is a real man." Tristan waved from behind his pint of IPA.

"A real man, like you…" She leaned in close and wound her fingers around his tie, pulling him to her. He swallowed and licked his lips. Precious yanked his tie, then released him, sending him flying off his stool. She laughed. "You couldn't handle me."

"So you don't want to come to the Christmas party with me?" Tristan asked in a careless tone from the floor, although his eyes looked serious. Did he have a thing for Precious?

"Nope. I'm going with Elle." She winked at me and turned to the bar. When she caught the bartender's eye, she held up two fingers. "Scotch. Two fingers."

"That's what she said." Tristan sprung back to his feet and held his hand up for a high five. Everyone ignored him.

"Disgusting," Precious sneered, and she walked over to give him a piece of her mind.

"So, how's your placement going?" I asked one of the other grads, a medium-height woman with brown skin and glossy hair. I hadn't spent a lot of time with the graduates since our induction at the fancy country house. Her name was Mandy…or Maud, something with an M.

"It's OK. I'm in internal audit, so it's good because I get to see a lot of the other parts of the company and make contacts. I'm thinking of choosing finance for my next placement." She paused to take a sip of her gin and tonic. It was the most I'd heard her say all night.

"Don't we get given our placements?" I furrowed my brow, trying to remember the details of the scheme.

"I mean, you can wait for an assignment, or you can network and use your initiative to get a placement somewhere you really want. What's Fae Audits like?"

"Er, it was pretty hardcore. We've been onsite in the fae realm, so there hasn't been a lot of time for networking." Her comments needled me. I should be out there, making a name for myself in other parts of the business.

I wished there was a fair playing field, where everyone knew all the rules and had the same chances with no surprises. Sometimes it seemed like I'd never understand all the social skills I needed to be successful.

The conversation with Albert floated to the front of my mind and, it might be crass, but I wanted to brag to this networker that I had opportunities too. "Actually, the director's so impressed, he's thinking of offering me a permanent job."

Her nose crinkled. "Really? Are you going to take it? You'd miss out on learning about different areas and all the education that comes with the grad scheme."

That hadn't even crossed my mind. "I could still do the courses."

"Maybe, but won't you be too busy with a permanent role?"

"I haven't said yes yet." Technically, I hadn't been offered a job yet.

"I think I'd choose to stay on the scheme, keep my options open for a bit longer before settling into a permanent role. I mean, how many jobs do you get where you can cycle through four placements in two years and get all that experience?"

I sipped my drink, ignoring her rhetorical question.

"So, did you get the invite to the Selection?"

"Yep." I'd received the invite to the Reaping last week. The gold lettering had shimmered against the black expensive card:

Miss Noelle Bruma,

You are cordially invited to attend the Graduate Scheme Selection Event to take place at sunset in the Board room at the Bathory Corporation London Headquarters followed by the End of Year Event in the Conference Suite.

Do not be late.

Merissa Hope

Director of Human Resources

"And you're coming to the Christmas party after?"

I nodded. I didn't want to go to the party. I had so much studying to do and there was a course on presentation skills that would take us out of the office for two days in preparation for the Selection presentation, so I'd have work to catch up with too. Plus, I was dreading the course. Two days of presenting…I got nauseous just thinking about it.

"You two talking about the Christmas party? I've heard they are insane." Tristan had escaped from Precious, who was back to dancing with a couple of other grads.

"Insane? It's a work Christmas party, how bad can they get?" I asked.

He looked at me knowingly. "If you heard some of the stories I've heard, then you'd know."

"Like what?" I challenged.

Beside me Mandy's eyes had gone large, and round and she leaned forward, hungry for gossip.

"Like last year, they had to fire someone who got drunk and told Liz exactly what he thought of her. And I heard an executive was caught with a secretary in a supply room."

"Who's Liz?" I asked.

He snapped his fingers. "Keep up, Elle, Elizabeth Bathory. The CEO."

I stared at him, unable to believe he had the gall to call her Liz as if she'd invited him into her inner sanctum and knew him like a friend. A horrible thought struck me; what if that was exactly what had happened? Maybe he did know her.

Everyone else was networking. Maybe it was just me who didn't understand how things worked. My head span. I wanted to go home.

I pushed my way through the dancers to tell Precious and knocked into someone; the bloke Precious had rejected at the bar. I looked up, intending to apologise, but he wasn't paying any attention to me. He had a screwed-up look of concentration on his face, directed at the dance floor. I saw a flash of something metallic in his hand. I blinked twice before my brain processed it. "Knife!"

Precious frowned at me, then her own dagger was in her palm. She struck out, knocking the would-be assailant to the floor. She knocked his wrist against the sticky dancefloor, sending the knife skidding away. I kicked it out of reach. No one around us noticed the altercation as everyone grinded up on each other.

I waved at a bouncer with a buzz cut who scanned the room. He frowned at me. I pointed at the fight going on next to me and he started making his way over.

"Orc scum," the man growled as he attempted to push Precious off. "You shouldn't be allowed in here."

"No means no, dzrakhead." She punched him in the side of the face, and he went still. She tucked her knife away somewhere under her skirt and stood, brushing herself down. She scowled at her top. "I'll never get that beer stain out."

The bouncer finally reached us. He gave Precious a look up and down.

She tensed, preparing for trouble.

"He had a knife," I said. "She was defending herself."

The bouncer considered this before nodding. "Then I expect there won't be any more trouble from you. Now get out."

Precious' nostrils flared and she looked like she was ready to fight him.

I dragged her back. "We're leaving."

Precious nodded and let me lead her away.

"Sorry," I said.

"You don't need to be sorry. He's the prick who moved on me at the bar. Some guys can't take no for an answer."

"Sorry you had to go through that," I amended.

Precious gave me a confused look and I could tell she genuinely didn't understand what I meant. But I hadn't seen such overt hate against supernaturals since I'd left school.

"For what he said," I tried again.

"Oh. When you're a supernatural, you get used to comments like that. It's nothing. I've had worse."

"But you shouldn't have to."

This time, her expression told me I was both ignorant and naïve. "Look, Elle, it's nothing. Some people are ignorant haters and that sucks, but I'd rather brush them off. The best revenge I can get is to do me, unapologetically, and get success. And things are getting better. There's a supernatural Member of Parliament now, and each generation gets more tolerant. Mostly. But, he's harshed my buzz. Let's get out of here."

"Actually, I'm heading home."

"I'll see you back safely," Precious offered.

"Nah, I'm good." Precious gave me a disbelieving look, like I couldn't handle myself on the London streets. Which, to be fair, I couldn't. But I had honed my London walk; head down, power forward, stop for no one. And I needed to get out of here. "Honest."

"OK. See you on Monday."

I waved goodbye and headed home. I debated taking the tube, but the knife loomed in my mind, so I stomped to the nearest taxi rank. The driver grumbled about going so far out of central London, but I must have looked pathetic enough that he agreed if I added an extra tenner to the fare. I nodded, too tired to argue, and settled in to listen to his lecture about the government, the price of fuel and the state of music nowadays. He pulled up next to a Lamborghini, a fancier car than I was used to seeing parked in our part of London, and I staggered out. I had barely uttered a thank you and he was off back to seek another fare.

Back home, I shouted out a hello to Abby. Silence. She must be out seeking her next conquest. I slumped on the sofa and turned my head so I could see Nibbles' cage. My scruffy hamster dug around in his food bowl before heading to his water bottle, then back to his food.

"Sometimes I envy you, Nibbles," I said to him. He gave a squeak and bared his teeth at me, before dashing into his red plastic house, stuffed to the brim with bedding. I frowned at a small grey feather that poked out of the organic shredded bedding and newspaper that he usually had. How did that get there?

I braved his teeth to retrieve it and then went to bed, going through my bedtime rituals with care. Sometimes, OK, most of the time, I wished I didn't care so much about the order, or the number of times I did something. What would it be like to be carefree and just flop into bed at the end of a weird day, like a normal person? But that wasn't me. And so, I smoothed make-up remover, cleanser, then toner, then moisturiser into my skin and massaged it into my face. Once I was satisfied I'd worked the product in, I turned off the light switch, then turned it on again. Lucky seven times. Guess I'd never know what normal felt like.

Chapter 37

Choose your appearance as carefully as you would select armour for battle.

Elizabeth Bathory – *The First Disrupter*

I went over my notes again. I'd practised my speech with Abby seven times. I knew. I'd counted.

"Put those away," Abby said as she picked through her extensive make-up tray. We were in the living room because it was larger than my bedroom and I didn't want the faint whiff of Nibbles' bedding seeping into my partywear. "You know it by heart."

Knowing the words wasn't the problem. It was saying them in front of a panel that made my stomach churn. The presentation course had been no help at all. I'd ended up mumbling at the floor when it was my turn, fidgeting with the Rubik's cube keyring in my pocket the whole time. The instructor used me as an example of what not to do. So, I just had to be the total opposite of myself, and I might get through the Reaping.

I should take some comfort knowing that Albert had said he'd vouch for me, but I still had to speak in front of a panel. I knew Newton would be there because he'd sent me an e-mail telling me not to disappoint him. No pressure.

I frowned at my reflection in the hand mirror and applied another layer of mascara like it was armour. "You're sure this isn't too much?" I planned to change into my party dress after the Reaping, but I needed Abby's help with my hair and make-up beforehand because there was no way I could pull off a party look in the company bathroom without help.

Abby appeared behind me. "Seriously? It's barely there. You're lucky you've got such good skin."

I moved to dab a spot of concealer over my birthmark, but Abby stopped me. "I've got a better idea." She led me into her bedroom and sat me down on her bed. I stroked the purple fur throw over her duvet, pulling the corners so they matched up with the edge of the bed.

"Here, now don't fidget."

"What are you doing?"

"You'll see."

"Wha–" I didn't like my friend's tone, but experience had taught me it was easier to go with her hare-brained schemes. It was only make-up, I could wipe it off on the tube if it was awful. So I closed my eyes and let her do her thing.

"Ta da!"

I blinked at the small mirror she held up to my face. She'd put silver glitter along my eyelids and over my birthmark, making it look like a small snowflake. I stared. It was beautiful. I'd never thought I could like the strange-shaped mark that marred my face, but she had transformed it into something ethereal and wonderful, something more than me and yet part of me. I reached up to touch it.

Abby swatted my hand away. "Don't ruin it."

"Abby…"

"I never understood why you try to hide your birthmark. It's beautiful and so are you. Now, where's your phone? We need a pre-party picture of you before some hot totty at work smears your make-up with all the snogging."

"Abby!"

"It's a work party. I know what goes on at those things, do you know how many letters I get about them in January? Don't roll your eyes at me, just promise me you'll have fun."

I threw my arms around my friend. "Thank you."

"What's this for?"

"The make-up, for putting up with me, for everything." I choked and tears welled up. What had I done to deserve such a good friend?

"Do not cry." Abby shook my shoulders gently before tucking the long strand of hair I left loose to cover my blemish behind my ear. "Or I'll cry and you'll ruin your eyes and you'll be late to the party. Now, phone."

She held her hand out, and I took three deep breaths to calm my emotions and force the tears back before handing over my phone. I stood and posed while she clicked away before she came and stood next to me, snapping some selfies. Laughing, she unlocked my phone and flicked through them, sending copies to herself.

Abby paused. "I don't think I've had an orc before…"

I looked over her shoulder and saw she had gone through all the photos of us and had moved onto the pictures of my work night out with Precious and the other grads.

"She's not a piece of meat, Abby. She's my work friend."

"OK, I'll back off. But if she has any friends…"

I rolled my eyes. "I'll ask."

"You're the best." She carried on scrolling through my phone before chucking it back to me. "Looks like a fun night, but you have some boring pictures on there."

I glanced down at the last photo. It was the one of the contract I had managed to take before Skathi caught us in his office. Might as well bin it, but something caught my eye. The signature was familiar.

"Oh no…"

Everything fell into place and I gripped my phone so tightly that my knuckles turned white. Abby frowned at me.

"Is everything OK?"

No. Everything was not OK. I now knew that someone at the Bathory Corporation had aided with Skathi's fraud, countersigning the collateralised loans so he could buy up maple syrup. I knew why Albert had watched me so closely the past few weeks, and I knew I had to tell someone as soon as possible. The anti-money laundering video had been clear on that.

Elizabeth Bathory would be at the party tonight, so it was the best time. I should go straight to the top with this. Except it might mean making a scene and that filled my stomach with butterflies, if the butterflies were the size of dragons and frying my insides with their flaming acid breath. But first I had to get through the Reaping.

Chapter 38

After your first placement, there will be a selection process where you will present your achievements to date and answer questions from a panel. Only if you pass this process, will you move on to your second placement.

Bathory Corporation Graduate Scheme Handbook

I marched past the single protestor still waving her sign outside the company's headquarters. I had bigger things to worry about than getting accosted with a lecture on why vampires were evil. It was almost ironic, because the bad guy here was my human boss.

I left my outfit for the party in the bathroom along with other suit carriers that the female graduates had placed there and made my way across the atrium to the lifts that would take me to the Boardroom. Liam stepped out of the lift, heading to the conference suite on the ground floor where the party had already started. His formal suit made him look even more handsome than in his daywear. I swallowed.

"You sure you want to do this?" he asked, holding the lift doors open for me to walk in.

"This is all I've ever wanted," I whispered.

"Then, good luck," he said. "I'll see you at the party on the other side." He let the doors close, watching me as if he wanted to say something else.

I blinked back the sudden surge of swirling emotions. I had to concentrate. I had to get through the Reaping and speak to Elizabeth. It was good to have goals.

I jigged my foot as I waited for my name to be called. There was no system. It wasn't alphabetical. It wasn't done by placements. I couldn't work it out. Normally, that would annoy me, but today I was too focused on rehearsing my speech.

All of the twenty graduates had different ways of letting out their nerves; Precious clenched and unclenched her fists, Tristan annoyed everyone by making stupid jokes. I bounced my foot up and down, arms crossed tight over my chest.

Merissa Hope, the HR Director, called our names one by one and people entered the Boardroom, stayed for a few minutes, then left the room either smiling or frowning with disappointment. One man ran out in floods of tears. That didn't help my nerves.

Precious got called before me. I mouthed 'good luck' at her and she gave me a thumbs up. After an eternity, she walked back out of the door.

"How did it go?" I asked.

She held out her fist for me to bump. "Nailed it."

Merissa called my name.

"I'll wait for you," said Precious, settling back into her seat.

I took a sip from my water bottle and went in. I froze by the door. Elizabeth Bathory was here. I knew she'd be at the end-of-year do, but I hadn't expected her to take the time to listen to the graduate presentations. Should I blurt out what I knew now?

"Noelle Bruma?" Elizabeth asked, shooting me a smile that exposed her fangs. "Please, take the stand and tell us why we should keep you on the graduate scheme."

OK. Now was not the time.

I stepped up to the lectern that had been placed in front of the large screen at one end of the Boardroom. A camera blinked at me behind Elizabeth. This was being recorded. Great.

My gaze took in the panel. Too many people. My stomach lurched. Newton's eyes narrowed. My gaze lit on Albert, who tipped his head to one side and gave me a sympathetic smile.

Seeing him sitting there thinking he could get away with fraud was enough to clear my head. I had to get through this so I could do the right thing and tell someone what he'd done. The swirling in my stomach eased enough that I could talk without the risk of vomiting.

I swallowed, straightened my shoulders, picked a point above Elizabeth's head to talk at so I didn't have to make eye contact, and began. "As you know, my first placement has been in Fae Audits, where I've been heavily involved in an audit of the fae realm…"

I worked my way through my prepared speech, barely glancing at the notecards I clutched in my hands. Abby was right; I had memorised what I needed to say. I covered my contribution to the team, my attention to detail, my dedication to the job and the company and touched on my stellar performance in my exams to date.

By the end, my throat was dry, but I'd made it. Now I just needed to figure out how to speak to Elizabeth alone.

The panel threw me a few questions about how I prioritised and why I thought I was a good fit for the company, which I'd prepared for, although I still stumbled over my responses.

I readied myself to get dismissed so they could decide my future, when to my horror, they started talking about my strengths and weaknesses in front of me. Crap. They would make the decision while I watched on, not hiding what they said about me.

I screwed up the notecards. This was torture.

Elizabeth turned to Newton. "Newton, you're her mentor. What do you think?"

"She has aptitude for the work and has displayed an admirable fortitude and determination. I vote 'aye'."

"And Albert?" Elizabeth asked.

"I think with the right role model, she'll be good. I'd be happy to have her as a permanent employee in my team."

Albert smiled at me.

I clenched my teeth. He wanted me where he could keep an eye on me and make sure I didn't blurt out anything about his role in the fraud. That conversation where he'd practically offered me a job made a lot more sense now; it was nothing to do with my skills and everything to do with covering his butt. I had to take him down. I opened my mouth.

Elizabeth wrote something in her notebook. "Noelle, you may stay on the graduate scheme. Congratulations and enjoy the party. We will inform you of your second placement within the next two weeks."

"May I say something?" I squeaked.

She raised her eyes to mine. "It is unusual for graduates to have something to add when they have already got the place. Please be quick, we have another five candidates to see."

I froze. Albert leaned forward and narrowed his eyes. *Did he know that I knew?* I couldn't do it. Not in front of everyone. "Thank you for the opportunity." I fled the room. Coward. I leaned against the wall in the waiting area and tried to slow my breaths.

"Bad luck," said Tristan. "Just don't vomit everywhere this time."

"I'm still on the scheme," I said through gritted teeth.

"Really?" he replied, not bothering to hide his surprise.

Merissa called his name, and he disappeared into the Boardroom.

"Let's wait until you're ready before we go to the party."

Precious helped me into a seat and rubbed my back.

Minutes later Tristan danced out, holding his hand out for high fives. "See you upstairs, suckers!" He bounded off.

I waited in the seat until everyone had finished. I could speak to Elizabeth after the panels, get her alone.

But her Executive Assistant walked through the waiting area before the assessors left the room and glared at us. "Clear out."

"I need to speak to Elizabeth. It's important."

"Everybody thinks they're important. It's my job to make sure Elizabeth isn't bothered by graduates who want to plead with her for a bigger role."

"But this is really important–"

"Not as important as the call with the Prime Minister." His voice turned sympathetic, "I understand that's frustrating for you, but you need to scoot," he waved us away, his eyes glowing slightly. What was with the assistants here? It was like they fed off people getting annoyed…

"It's fine." Precious tugged me to the lifts.

The assistant turned his back on us.

"I could have convinced him," I protested.

Precious shoved me into the elevator. "You want to speak to the CEO."

"Yes. That's why I was talking to her EA." Did I have to spell it out?

Precious nodded. "We'll catch her at the party."

Chapter 39

Dear Abby, I don't want to go to my work's Christmas party. I don't really like the people I work with and I don't want to spend my free time with them, but I'm worried that if I don't go, it will look bad. What should I do?

Honey, I love a good office Christmas party; the food, the decorations... the office scandals, but this isn't about me, this is about you. So, let's thought cake this thing. You feel you have to go because you're worried about how it will look (icing thought), but there's more to life than work and you can absolutely spend your free time how you choose – if you need permission, this is me giving it to you. And if you want a valid excuse, then food poisoning is a good one that doesn't get any follow up questions.

But maybe there's more here. If you can't stand your colleagues enough to spend one evening with them (that's the first layer thought), maybe you're in the wrong job and you feel stuck there with no prospects and no joy (there – that's your gooey centre). But I get it, peer pressure is hard. So, if you still feel you have to go, enjoy the free food and drink and have a friend call you after an hour with an excuse and that's your out. Who knows, you might even enjoy it and have an office romance!

Yours cakefully, Abby.

Abby Wright – *Ask Abby*

I smoothed my dress down and entered the conference suite. Precious had told me to leave her while she finished transforming into a party goddess so I was alone. Blue and silver balloons hung suspended from the ceiling and silver streamers looped between them. A large banner read: *Merry Christmas from the Bathory Corporation* over a stage where a band played.

A few people danced to the music, others hovered by the buffet table. Edwyn sat alone at a large circular table, staring at a drink. I took a breath and headed over to him. I could at least try to mend one relationship here before I destroyed the Fae Audits team.

"Merry Christmas."

He turned his head a fraction of an inch so he could see me and grunted, "Merry Christmas."

I coughed and placed a shiny bag on the table.

"What's this?" he sighed.

"A Christmas present."

He sat back in his chair and regarded me. "And I didn't get you anything." His voice was heavy with sarcasm.

I shrugged. "A peace offering then." I didn't want any enemies at the company, and if I could screw up the courage to expose Albert, Edwyn might end up taking over the department. He could be my boss one day, perish the thought, and I should try to get on his good side.

He quirked his head, his curiosity piqued, and opened the gift. His lips twitched and threatened to form a smile as he held the bag of Goblin Blend caramel coffee beans.

"I assume you have a grinder."

He nodded.

"Well…merry Christmas." I stood.

"Wait." He inhaled deeply, opened his mouth to say something, then reformed it. "You're alright, Bruma."

I nodded and grinned back at him. It wasn't an apology, but it was the best I'd get from Edwyn, and maybe now we could have some sort of truce.

"You too, Winnie."

He laughed at that. "Go enjoy your first Bathory Christmas party. And stay away from the punch; it's been spiked."

I left while he was still playing nice and skirted the room, looking for someone I recognised. I caught sight of Precious and waved. She strode over, her burgundy dress making her green skin look luscious. Her hair hung in long, twisted braids down her back. Gold beads threaded in them caught the light from the mirror ball spinning in the middle of the room. How she'd done that while all I'd done was change from my suit into a dress, I'd never know.

"Hey girl, you look good."

"Thanks." I gave her a twirl so she could take in the dress Abby had picked out for me. Navy blue, thin fabric with a ruffled hem that fell to just below my knees. Somehow it even made me look like I had curves, although that may have been the lacy push-up bra that she insisted I buy to go with the outfit. "You look amazing!"

She spun for me, her scarlet dress fanning out around her like she was in a movie. "Tell me how I can help." Precious switched to business mode so fast it took me a minute to catch up with her.

"It's OK. I'm going to talk to Elizabeth. This is big, so I need to make sure it goes way above Albert. I just need to get her alone."

"She's giving a speech." Precious nudged me, and I saw the CEO of the Bathory Corporation walk onto the stage with confident steps.

"Perfect. I'll wait until she's done then talk to her before she starts mingling."

"Good luck."

I nodded to Precious and edged around the large hall to the stage as Elizabeth Bathory started her speech. My stomach was caught in a tornado inside me, and I forced myself to breathe. I was only going to speak to her. One person. This was not a presentation. She was just a person. My inspiration. And the CEO of the company I worked for. And a powerful vampire. But underneath that, she was just a person.

Besides, I'd survived the Reaping. This was a piece of cake.

My hands itched, and I tapped my thumbs to each of my fingers in turn as I waited for her to finish her speech.

"Welcome, everyone, to our Christmas party. I'm so happy to see you all here and equally happy to say that we have surpassed our revenue forecasts this quarter thanks to a few diligent teams, including our audit department, so a round of applause for them." The room erupted into clapping and I heard Tristan's voice whoop above the noise. "Now, I know I'm keeping you from food, and more importantly, the bar." She paused and a smattering of laughter filled the room. "So, I'll keep this brief. This is an opportunity for us all to unwind and let our hair down, but remember, you are still at work so I expect you to behave with some decorum. Merry Christmas, everyone."

She stepped down from the stage, and the musicians took up their instruments again. I swallowed and moved to intercept her before she could make it down the final step.

"Miss Bathory, ma'am, there's something I need to tell you." My voice echoed in my ears, but I carried on. "Albert Ahrenns, the Director of Fae Audits, he's involved in some serious fraud with the fae. I've got all the evidence on my phone." I showed her the picture of Albert's signature on the document confirming the fake stone's collateral.

There was a stunned silence. Even the music had stopped. Elizabeth Bathory unhooked her microphone and held it out. With a blur of speed, an assistant zoomed over and pocketed it. I stared around the room. All eyes were on me. A wave of nausea flooded through my stomach. Everyone had heard.

"Thank you for bringing this to my attention. I will make sure we look into it as a matter of urgency."

I nodded, clamped a hand over my mouth, and ran for the bathroom as the whispers began. I stayed in the toilet for twenty minutes. The initial vomiting was over quickly, but the anxiety and fear lingered in the pit of my stomach. Precious had come in to check I was alright, but I'd sent her away after accepting her offer of a breath mint. No one else needed their night ruined because of me.

Once my breathing had calmed and the anxiety in my stomach was a dull ache instead of a blazing dread, I decided to leave the safety of the bathroom. I would grab a drink and go home.

I scanned the dancefloor for Precious and saw her grinding against Tristan, of all people. I considered going over to check she was alright and he hadn't slipped something in her drink, but she seemed to be the one in control judging by the intense way he looked at her while she moved in time with the beat. Happy she was OK and not wanting to interrupt whatever buzz she had going on, I headed for the bar, ordered a glass of water and took a second breath mint from the sympathetic bartender. I took a slow drink, enjoying how it cooled my burning throat.

"You made it then?"

I whirled round to see Liam leaning on the bar next to me, a tight smile playing on his lips. My face crinkled in confusion.

"Your first placement. And the Reaping. You survived."

I nodded. Survival was one word for it.

"And your performance up there was something else."

A blush heated my face. "Glad I could provide the entertainment." My voice came out husky. That might have been the result of the earlier vomiting.

He laughed. "Is outing corporate fraudsters all you can do?"

"What did you have in mind?" Was this a trap? Because this almost sounded flirty.

"How about a dance?"

I sipped my water, nodded and took his hand. I might as well enjoy a dance before I fled, after all, the fraud was in the CEO's hands now and I'd already made a fool of myself. Nothing else bad could happen tonight.

Liam led me onto the dance floor and we bopped in time to the final few seconds of an upbeat song before the tempo changed and the band played a slower, more romantic number. I looked around.

Precious had moved closer to Tristan and held him in a slow dance pose. He looked like Christmas had come early as she swayed him in time with the music.

I coughed, nerves seizing me, but Liam took hold of my hands and placed them on his shoulders. I gave him a shy smile. He moved his hands to my waist, skimming the silky fabric of my dress. I stared at his chest before risking a glance at his face. That small smile played over his lips as he met my gaze.

I looked away. It was too intimate. A compulsion seized me. I had to check in on Abby. I forced it down, allowing my hands to tap his muscular shoulders three times, to the beat of the music so he didn't think I was a total weirdo.

The song ended, but he didn't release me, the heat of his hands spread through my skimpy dress and pooled in my stomach. What was happening?

"Elle." My name was a caress on his lips, full of promise and questions.

"Liam, there you are," a female voice said.

Liam sighed as he stepped away. "Elle, this is Rani, my girlfriend."

The woman shook back her mane of hair and held out a hand to me, her multitude of rings glinting under the glitterball.

My stomach sank. Of course he had a girlfriend. What was I thinking? That we'd had a moment? Naïve fool. Besides, I had more important things to worry about. The compulsion surfaced again. I'd left the oven on, and Abby wouldn't notice, so the flat would fill up with toxic smoke and she'd die from carbon monoxide poisoning because I hadn't checked the batteries since last month and then her body would be consumed by flames, and I'd lose the only person who cared about me. Water would make it better. Water fought fire. I had to get to some taps.

"I have to go," I muttered and ran for the toilets, leaving him confused on the dancefloor.

Chapter 40

I've come up against my fair share of adversaries in my business. They all have one thing in common; they only respect strength.

Elizabeth Bathory – *The First Disrupter*

Safely inside the ladies' loo, I chose a sink – although choose is a strong word when the compulsion drove me to pick one – and turned the taps on and off in a stuttering pattern. It calmed me a little. Now I just needed to check Abby was alive. I rang Abby. Pick up, please pick up, don't be dead because I didn't turn the oven off.

"How's the party going?" she answered on the second ring.

"Did I turn the oven off?"

"You didn't cook today."

"I know. But I have to know. Please, Abby."

"OK." I could feel her rolling her eyes through the phone.

"I'm walking to the oven and it is off."

"Are you sure?"

"Sending you proof." My phone buzzed and a wave of relief washed over me as I saw the oven was indeed off. She sent more pictures. It wasn't as good as checking myself. But it was enough to calm me, for now. But I should probably just go home.

"Hang up the phone, Noelle."

I whirled round. Albert stood in the ladies' toilets, hammy hands clenched into fists.

"What are you doing here?" I'd never seen a man in the ladies before. And he was the manager I'd just blown the whistle on to Elizabeth Bathory.

"Elle? Are you OK?" Abby's voice sounded through the phone.

He dashed at me and had the phone out of my hand before I could think. With a mean smile, he hung up and threw it into a sink. I edged forward, but he spun and pressed me against the wall. The tiles were cool through the thin fabric of my dress. Sweat pooled in the small of my back. The shock of seeing him had cut through the compulsions, though, so at least I could think straight as he loomed over me.

"You've made my life very difficult, Noelle. I had a good thing going with those deals."

"They would have spotted your seal, eventually. It was only a matter of time."

He shook his head, his eyes were two furious gimlets boring

into mine. "No, they wouldn't. It was perfect. I swapped out the documents for ones without my name."

I frowned. "When?"

"When you handed them to me outside the mansion, and I went to tell the others you were alright. I swapped them out for ones I had prepared. You were getting too close."

"Why?" I choked out as his bulk pressed against my chest.

He gave me a look like I was the stupidest person he'd met. When he spoke, his sour breath brushed my face. "Money. What else? Skathi paid me to sign off the fake collateral, a percentage of the gold he could get from the emperor by selling him back the maple syrup he'd bought at an inflated price. Faes are weird. They need enough in reserve for…It doesn't matter. I had enough to buy me a nice place somewhere tropical with lots of daylight, away from these bloody vampires. But now…" His dark eyes were full of hatred. I flinched from the force of it. "Now, you have made things very difficult. The entire company is looking for me and they've frozen my assets. So, you can take back what you said."

I shook my head, dumbly.

Albert sighed. "If you need an incentive…" His hands wrapped around my throat, and I made a small squeak. "People have died at these parties before. I don't want to do it, but I need you to tell them you made a mistake so I can get my life back." Get his money back, more like.

I scrabbled at his fleshy arms, but his grip tightened, choking off my air. My vision blurred to black around the edges. I clawed at his unmoving hands in desperation.

I tried to speak, and he released his hands a little. "I already showed her the photos," I squeaked.

"You can say you fabricated the evidence."

"Why would I do that?"

Albert's eye twitched. "Who knows why attention-seeking graduates do these things? You wanted to prove yourself or maybe you wanted a promotion. It doesn't matter," his fingers tightened around my neck again, "you just need to tell everyone that you made a mistake and I can leave here without having a horde of bloody vampires tracking me down.

"I know what you're thinking, you're thinking that you've got too much honour to take back your accusation. You think you know how the world works but you've got no idea about anything. So, I'll enlighten you. You are nothing special, you're a stupid little girl swimming with sharks. And if you don't change your story, I'll hurt your friends. You're close to Precious, I think I'll deal with her first. A few anonymous complaints ought to get her fired and then she can crawl back to whatever rock orcs live under.

"And then there's your flatmate. Abby, isn't it? You're close, aren't you? You've lived together since the second year of university. Don't look so surprised, I listen to my team's talk. She'll be all alone in your shoebox apartment, feeling safe…well, you get the picture. So, it's your choice. What are you going to do?"

He released the pressure on my throat enough that I could suck in a breath and croak out an answer. I tried to think through the fog of fear that clouded my mind. "Will they believe me?"

"Of course they will. You're on a graduate scheme, barely three months into your first real job. You made a mistake. A stupid mistake. I've been here for twenty years. What's more plausible? You making a mistake or a dedicated director committing fraud?"

I nodded.

"Don't worry, it'll only be one mark on your employee record. You won't be fired. I'll keep you close. Make the call. Now." He removed one of his hands and pulled a phone from his pocket. As he pulled up the number, my mind reeled.

A mark on my employee record. Permanently. For telling the truth. The unfairness of it hit me like a brick wall. I didn't want this. I didn't want him to win. Without thinking, I lifted my knee sharply into his groin. He bent over, wheezing and released his grip on my throat. If I was going to leave the company, I'd do it on my own terms.

But I'd survived six foster homes, and I wasn't going to let him bully me out. Resolve stiffened my stomach. I stamped on his instep, my heel grinding into his bones with a meaty crunch. I scooped up my phone from the sink and fled.

Straight into Newton. He curled his lip at me. "Elle?"

My mouth moved, but I couldn't get any sound out. My throat felt thick and bruised and my whole body trembled from the adrenaline. Newton tilted his head to one side. "Your heart is racing." He looked from the bathroom door to me and raised an eyebrow.

I could follow the train of his thoughts, and heat flooded my face. No, no, no. I wasn't the type of person who had sex in an employee bathroom.

"It's not like that," I tried to say, but my voice was barely a whisper, my throat crushed and sore. He pushed back the strands of my hair that had fallen out of my chignon and stared at my neck. I pushed his hand away. No vampire would get their fangs into my neck. Not even my mentor. Not today.

"What happened?" His voice was low and dangerous. I hung my head. He cocked his head as if listening. "There's another heartbeat in there. Who did this to you?"

The adrenaline left me, and a cold sensation filled me instead. I couldn't say his name. He'd kill me. Not only me, everyone I cared about. I swallowed. I should have walked away. I should have taken him up on his offer. Newton lifted my chin with his forefinger and forced me to meet his gaze, his eyes glowing red.

"Tell me."

I opened my mouth, but there was too much at stake. I wouldn't betray Precious and Abby by blabbing.

The bathroom door swung open, and Albert appeared, framed in the fluorescent light of the ladies' toilets. Newton's eyes narrowed, and he sped over with inhuman speed, crushing Albert against the wall.

Chapter 41

One always has a choice. Often it is a choice between mediocrity and greatness.

Elizabeth Bathory – *The First Disrupter*

I ran through the enormous ballroom, lifting my skirt up around my thighs so my legs could move faster and propel my body out of this hell. I pushed my way through two sets of double doors and collapsed against the rough but cool wall outside, gulping in the fresh night air like I was drowning.

My entire body trembled, and I hugged my arms around my waist, suddenly cold. I sank to the ground, hearing my new dress rip as it snagged on the stone. Torn. Like me. I lifted my knees up and wrapped my arms around them, forcing myself into a ball and pressing my eyes into my legs, blocking out everything else.

How had everything I'd wanted gone so wrong? The

Bathory Corporation was tough, but I'd done well, I'd come to the attention of management, been considered for a promotion, even found some work friends. I'd started to belong. But, like every other time I'd felt like I might finally be able to put down some roots, this would be snatched away from me too.

Newton had probably killed Albert. I'd made a fool of myself in front of the entire company, and now I'd have to leave before I was sacked. A small sob escaped me.

"Have a tissue." The kind voice next to me made me jump. I looked up through red-ringed eyes, leaving swirls of mascara and glitter on my legs and dress to see the lone protestor holding out a packet of tissues.

"Thank you." I took it. The good Samaritan rested against their protest sign. Just what I needed, a lecture on how evil the Bathory Corporation was.

"Are you alright?"

I shook my head. "Everything's gone wrong."

She nodded and offered me a thermos flask of steaming tea. I shook my head. She shrugged and poured herself a cup, which she held in her gloved hands.

"It's a bit cold to be protesting, isn't it?" I asked, wiping my eyes and nose with the tissue.

The protestor looked around and I got the impression she could see further than the glass-fronted buildings that surrounded us.

"Sometimes you have to take a bit o' pain for what you

believe in."

Insightful, but not much help to me. I made some sort of disbelieving noise and she snapped her head back to face me, her cold eyes capturing mine as if they could see deep into the depths of my soul.

"You're troubled."

"That's not the half of it."

"Tell me."

I sighed. Why not? What had I got to lose? It wasn't like I could stay at the Bathory Corporation, so I might as well break another one of their rules and chat with the protestor. "Well, I found out that someone committed fraud, and reported it to everyone, damaging my boss's reputation as well as the company's, then I assaulted my boss in the women's toilets and I think my mentor might have killed him. And I'll probably be fired."

She blinked at me and took another sip of tea, considering. "So, what're your choices?"

"Choices? I don't have any choices." I fisted my hands and pressed them against my eyes until I could see red sparks flash across my closed eyelids.

"Nonsense. You always have a choice. The only question is; what do you believe in?"

I waited three seconds before I opened my eyes. What the hell sort of question was that? I opened my mouth to tell her that, but she was gone. I looked around, but there was no sign of the woman, her mismatched knitwear, her faded thermos, or her cardboard protest sign.

Choice. What choice did I have? I was about to be fired for assault or gross misconduct or ruining the precious reputation of the Bathory Corporation and then I'd have to slink back to the supermarket that had offered me a part-time job stacking shelves, I'd never get my accounting qualification without experience in the field and, after months of barely scraping by with rent and bills, Abby would kick me out and wouldn't speak to me again. My life was ruined.

I heaved out another sob. Not even picking out the frayed threads on my expensive dress helped ease the anxiety.

But then, as I plucked another thread, a small spark of courage kindled somewhere deep inside of me. There were times I'd spiralled before. Dark times in worse situations than this. I still had prospects.

Graduate schemes were well known for their pressure. The dropout rate was fifty per cent for Bathory's graduate scheme alone. So, maybe another firm wouldn't hold that against me. And I'd started my qualification and passed the first three exams, so that put me officially at 'part-qualified', another firm might like that I didn't have to start from scratch.

And, my mind skirted round to the big truth; I hadn't done anything wrong. I had followed the proper procedures, reported fraud where I had found it and, dammit, I had integrity. So, if they were going to fire me, I could tell…someone. Abby had press contacts, and the Bathory Corporation could shove it where the sun didn't shine.

My spine straightened, and I pushed myself upright. I might not have any choice over whether I still had a job after tonight, but I darn well had a choice over how I reacted. I could slink away and cower, or I could stride back in and face them all with my head held high. And if they fired me, I would tell them exactly what I thought of the whole stupid company.

Chapter 42

The Archives contains all the knowledge the company possesses and is also used to house artefacts that the company protects on behalf of our clients. Do not go there unattended.

Bathory Corporation Employee Handbook

I strode back in, but my entrance was ruined when I stumbled into someone in a sequinned black dress.

"Too much to drink?" Kylie's cruel laugh sounded loud in my ears. Great. Of course I had to run into my assigned buddy tonight. I walked past her.

"Can't handle the job, can't handle the drink," she taunted. "What can you do?"

I whirled round. "Enough. I get it. You don't want to be friends. You don't want anything to do with me, so leave me alone. I've had a bad night. So, just eff off will you."

Her beautiful face sagged into a stunned expression that

made her look like a badly made doll. "Don't speak to me like that."

"Why? What are you going to do? Report me?" A bark of raspy laughter escaped my lips. I'd gone way past reports tonight and I didn't even care.

A delicate finger tapped me on the back. I spun round, not in the mood for whatever this was. "What?"

I froze in horror.

Elizabeth Bathory stood there wearing a dangerous expression that chilled my blood. Newton stood behind her, eyeing me, his lips tight as if he were suppressing a smile. Albert was nowhere to be seen. I lowered my eyes and mumbled an apology.

"I hear that we have you to thank, not only for exposing Albert, but for finding him too."

I nodded, unable to meet her gaze, shrinking back into myself in the face of the CEO.

"I understand this is difficult for you. If you want to leave the corporation, then, as a gesture of goodwill, I'll offer you three months' pay in lieu of your notice period and of course we will provide adequate references."

She waited while I processed this. I could leave. I could go and find another job, somewhere with less risk, where my boss didn't want to kill me and vampires didn't wait around every corner. Even better, I could leave with dignity and a decent safety net. It was tempting.

Or you could stay. Newton's words from our mentor

meeting rang through my mind; 'it's your choice, Elle, but I thought you were strong' merging with the words from the protestor outside. I had a choice. I always had a choice.

"You're not firing me?" I squeaked out.

Elizabeth laughed, a brittle sound like she didn't do it a lot. "Gracious me, no. You found a significant fraud and the fae emperor will be very pleased with this. You've still got a place on the graduate scheme, if you want it."

I wasn't being fired.

Confidence filled me, straightening my spine. I was made of stronger stuff. I had survived the foster system and got a job everyone thought was out of my reach. I wouldn't let anyone push me around anymore. This was my decision and, crazy as it was, it felt right here. I'd survived. Despite fae monsters and frauds and a homicidal boss, I'd done it. I'd made it to the second placement on the most exclusive graduate scheme in the UK.

I belonged here. I would succeed here and prove myself no matter what. And I wasn't going to let anyone push me out.

I squared my shoulders and lifted my face until I could look her straight in her dark red eyes. I shook my head. "I'm staying."

"Congratulations." A ghost of a smile crossed her face. "I admire your courage. And I have the perfect next placement for you; the Archives." With that, Elizabeth Bathory swept away, leaving me gaping after her.

"The Archives?" A giggle made my head turn.

I sighed and took a step away from Kylie. She'd heard the whole thing. Obviously.

"Is that where your next placement is? You must have really screwed up."

"Why? What's the Archives?"

"Only the worst department in the company."

~

Thank you for reading Vampire Graduate Scheme – Placement One: Fae Audits. If you'd like to read a bonus chapter of the assessment centre from Liam's point of view, you can find it here:

And you can get a prequel to the series and find out how Elle meets Nibbles here:

Thank you

A special thank you to my amazing patrons: Emma Ward, ZomBev, Mark Canty and Sueann Snow who always support me.

If you want to support Gemma, you can find her on www.patreon.com/G_Clatworthy for exclusive first reads of new stories.

You can also join her newsletter at www.gemmaclatworthy.com for free stories and follow Gemma on www.instagram.com/gemmaclatworthy, www.facebook.com/gemmaclatworthy or join the Facebook reader's group; Gemma's book wyrms.

Other Books by G Clatworthy

Vampire Graduate Scheme series:

Placement One: Fae Audits

Placement Two: The Archives

Placement Three: Executive Assistant

Books set in the same universe as Vampire Graduate Scheme:

Rise of the Dragons series:

Awakening

Solstice of Dragons

Equinox Betrayal

Darkest Deception

Attack on Avalon

Fated Bloodlines

Eat, Pray, Dragons

Magical Liaison Office (a short story collection)

Omensford series:

Bedsocks and Broomsticks

Cream Teas and Crystal Balls

Donkeys and Demons

Pumpkins and Popstars

Exes and Enchantments

Fae and Familiars

Gnomes and Necromancy

Children's Books

The Child Who series:

The Girl Who Lost Her Listening Ears

The Boy Who Lost His Listening Ears

The Girl Who Dreamed of Sleep

The Boy Who Dreamed of Sleep

Nanny Pastry series:

Nanny Pastry and the Nimble Ninjabread Man

Other books:

Coronavirus in the words of children

About the Author

Gemma started writing during the 2020 lockdown and loves fantasy fiction and dragons in particular. She lives in Wiltshire with her family and two cats and enjoys crafts of all kinds. You can read all her writing first on www.patreon.com/G_Clatworthy.

Or join the conversation at Gemma's book wyrms readers' group on Facebook.

She also writes children's books. You can find out more on her website www.gemmaclatworthy.com or follow her on Instagram (www.instagram.com/gemmaclatworthy) or Facebook (www.facebook.com/gemmaclatworthy).

www.gemmaclatworthy.com